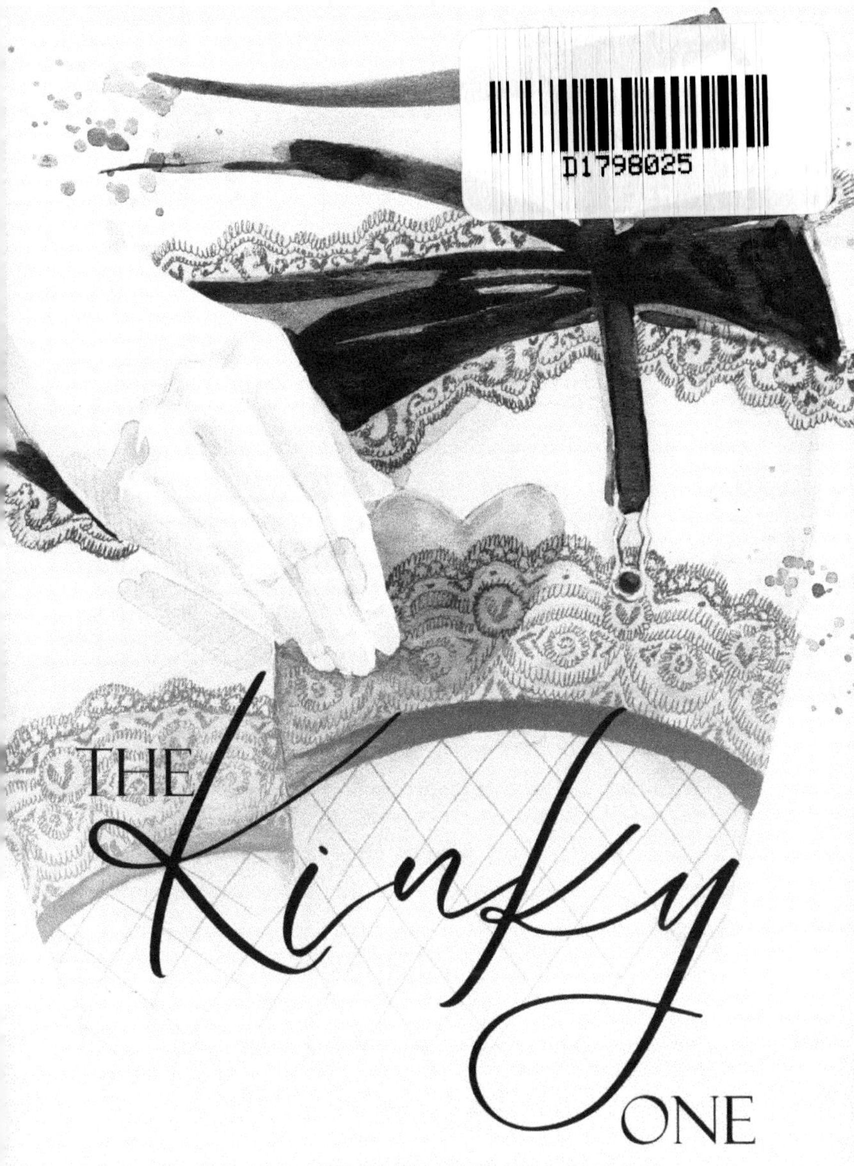



# THE Kinky ONE

THE ESCORT SERIES VOLUME 2

N.O. ONE

The Kinky One – Book 2 of The Escort Series



Cover design – Jo Armitage

Editing – Encompass Press Ltd

Published by Hudson Indie Ink & N.O. One

www.hudsonindieink.com

www.author-no-one.com

The Kinky One, N.O. One – 2nd ed.

ISBN-13: 978-1-917471-01-5

# Warning / Foreword

**Before you continue...**

**The Kinky One is the second volume of a series of six.**

It is graphic and morally on the fence, containing extremely sensitive material that may not be adapted to your needs.

If you need specific details of things involved, please visit our website for a list of warnings.

www.author-no-one.com

If you're okay with all of this, just remember... we warned you.

On the plus side, the lead female is strong and proud and these men come with a fire extinguisher.

If you're still reading after all of that then, by all means, sit down, relax, and enjoy the filthy, bumpy road ahead.

To reiterate:

**!! If you have triggers, please do not continue. This is not the series for you. !!**

Seriously, if you don't want all the angst and smut with some suspenseful darkness thrown in for good measure, stop reading.

Did you stop?

No?

Excellent! You're now one of us and we have claimed you as our own, you filthy rebel you ;)

This is for anyone who ever believed in us. And all of the inspiring sexy bitches of the world.

And let's not forget New York City... she's the most inspiring bitch of all.

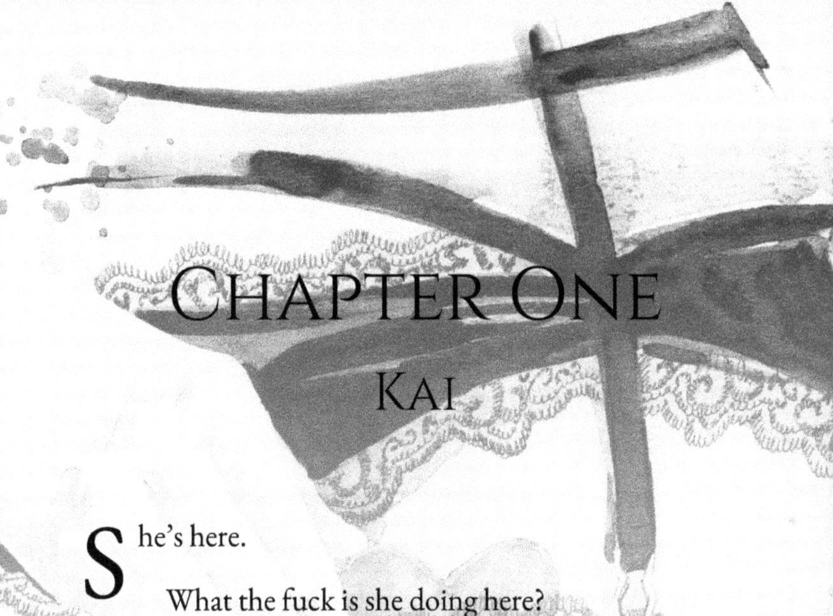

# Chapter One

## Kai

She's here.

What the fuck is she doing here?

Our eyes lock, her green ones boring into mine. In them, I can see the questions, and something I wish I could explain.

I cringe as Freya passes her, chirpily pointing out the obvious. "River, we didn't think you'd be here." The sarcastic response River wants to let out is held back by pure will, it's in the twist of her lips and the tightening of her jaw as she masks her true feelings with a smile for Freya.

"Some fucked up shit happened, so she's staying with us for a bit."

*What the fuck is that supposed to mean?*

Eyes darting to River's as Everest explains why she's here, my blood heats and boils over. Every muscle in my body tenses as my fists clench by my sides. All I want to know is what happened to my Psyche. I've got a million questions but I can't ask them because I've dug myself into a fucking huge hole with Freya. Schooling my features, I scan every inch of River, hoping I don't find anything that'll make me lose my mind. Like a wound or a bruise. The mere thought of my girl in pain physically hurts.

No, not my girl… not anymore.

"Oh, well, maybe the news will cheer you up, then."

Shit. Here it comes. Freya is practically vibrating with excitement, and my body heats. I didn't want Psyche to find out this way. I planned to talk to her about it all, explain what's going on. She would have probably talked me out of it and come up with a much better solution, but my fucking bullheadedness screwed me.

River folds her arms across her chest and glares at me, daring me to give her this great news. I really don't want to but I've made a promise and I'm nothing if not loyal. Besides, River isn't single anymore, she's somebody else's—and I'm the fucking idiot who let it happen. There's no denying she looked happy in those Page Six pictures. Even if she was fake as fuck and hiding her gorgeous short brown hair. The way one side is longer than the other and falls over her green eyes makes me want to go over there and tuck it behind her ear, using it as an excuse to gently caress her face with my thumb. Maybe even sneak in a little kiss on my favorite beauty mark.

Here's the thing... Freya and I have a history, although not the kind everyone thinks. We haven't corrected them because the reality of it all is worse than their imagination.

What started out as me being a loyal friend, has turned into a commitment I wasn't expecting. At the time, it made sense.

I could have found a better solution, but spite got the better of me and it was like my mouth went rogue. And now I wish I could take it back, but I can't. Actually, I won't. I'm not a *complete* bastard. When we finally got the news she had been waiting for, coupled with the shock of Tyler fucking Walker dating my girl, my mouth and brain disconnected.

Wrapping her arm around my waist and squeezing me closer to her, Freya holds out her left hand.

"We're getting married."

I can feel Freya's eyes looking up at me, but my gaze is solely fixed on River. Nothing could tear me away from her reaction as my heart pounds in my chest. A part of me wishes she would throw a fit, maybe a few insults, to show me she isn't okay with this. A part of me wishes she would break down and cry for *us*. For what we should have been.

But the bigger part of me would be disappointed in her for reacting with such dramatics. It's not her style, it goes against everything she is.

And, as always, she is true to herself.

The look in River's eyes is one of pain, disappointment, and is that anger? I can read my *gi...* my best friend's face like a book. Right now, I imagine it matches my own. She manages to school her features into a robotic smile—that I hate with every fiber of my being—as she congratulates us, and Everest hands her a glass of Petal's homemade bubbly.

Freya squeals with excitement as Everest pulls her in for one of his bear hugs, and Petal just looks at me with one eyebrow raised and a knowing expression. She shakes her head slightly before opening her arms up to me and bringing me in. Her tiny frame is swallowed up by my bulk as I gently squeeze her. She's disappointed, I get it. Petal's been rooting for River and me for years. It's like she has a sixth sense about these things and she always knows what we all want. What we all need. Anyone would think she'd be weak, but I know that underneath all those pixie features, she's a lioness. Fiercely protective of her family. I'm just lucky she thinks of me as one of them.

"So, when's the bachelor party?" Everest slaps me on the back as he clinks my glass with his. "Or are you going to be traditional and let the best man organize it?" He wags his eyebrows suggestively. Who my best man is going to be has never been a question in my mind. It's not a question in Ev's either. He knows it's him without me making some grand gesture.

I just always imagined my bride would eventually be his sister.

"You can let your freak flag fly, dude. It's all on you. Go wild." It's easy to smile with Ev. He pisses me the fuck off sometimes—he's so laid back, he's almost horizontal—but he's like a solid rock in an ever-flowing stream; always there and willing to do stupid shit with me.

Despite the feel-good vibes coming from him, sometimes, I just wish he'd step up a little more. Take more responsibility for himself and Petal. I swear to fuck, there are days it seems River is more his mother than his sister. She won't talk about it but I'd bet my left nut she has sacrificed a fuckload more than she's willing to tell us.

Every time we ask her how she can afford this or that...

Or when she put the down payment on their house and just shrugged it off like it was no big deal...

She just changes the subject and tells him not to worry about it.

So he doesn't. Because that's Everest fucking Fox. He takes everything at face value.

Living on the commune with our parents was crazy. Ev, River, Freya and I were inseparable. If I'm honest with myself, I always thought Ev would end up with Freya, but then we met Petal at a festival and he's been hers ever since. The way they look at each other with so much love reminds me of how River and I used to look at each other. I still see it sometimes, when she thinks I'm not paying attention, but she always hides it so quickly. Putting on that mask I see her use for other people. I hate it when it's directed at me.

Downing my glass of celebratory champagne feels soothing for all of two seconds. Freya hasn't stopped talking at Petal since she broke the news—yes, *at*... not to or with. Petal is clinging to Ev, making him endure the plans Freya has for our wedding. We're all enduring it, really. There's no room for anyone else to speak as she tells us how she'd like to get married on the beach with the waves crashing onto the sand.

It sounds beautiful, it really does. And if this were a regular wedding between two people who are madly and unquestionably in love with each other, it would sound like the perfect day to seal a commitment. But it's not, and we've talked about this. I tried to make it as clinical as I could, but this is Freya. We've known each other our entire lives. She needs me. Her parents are traveling around the country and as much as they wanted to help her, they can barely afford the gas they put into that nineteen-ninety-two Four Winds RV. Hell, I had to fix it up and rebuild the bed inside before they left again or else it wouldn't have lasted from here to Jersey.

But as it stands, my thoughts are on the heartbreak I saw in River's eyes as Freya broke the news. Right now, I'm fucking relieved Freya wants to keep the truth from everyone until she feels the time is right, because I can't be in the room when River finds out. She knows me better than anyone and would know in an instant my reasons for marrying Freya aren't for love. It's too late to talk to her about it. Too late for other options.

I'm such a fucking coward.

Truth be told, I'm still stung about her dating a fucking mogul. And not just any billionaire asshole, either. No. Of course not. Eight million people in the city of New York, and she's fucking Forbes' most eligible bachelor. It's bullshit and I hate it, but at the end of the day, I'm just her best friend. Looking around the room, I mentally correct myself as I spot River walking up the stairs to the second floor, her face pale and tight.

Ex-best friend.

Fuck, I hope not.

"Anyone want a refill?" I manage to interrupt as Freya takes a breath, holding my glass up to the group.

"Oh let me do that for you, you should be celebrating, not waiting on us." Petal's eyes light up at the excuse to get away for a few minutes.

"I am celebrating, but it's okay, Pet. I can do it. I need the bathroom anyway, so I can bring refills on my way back."

"Oh don't be silly." Her voice is like honey, but her little doll eyes are murderous, telling with just one look that I need to let her do this. "You go and do your business and there'll be fresh drinks waiting when you come back. Want a refill, Bear?" Petal turns to her husband with eyes so full of love it's almost sickening as Freya tightens her hold around my waist.

"I'd like to refill you," he growls, nestling into Petal's neck. She giggles in response, gently pushing him away as she tries to compose herself.

"Ev!"

He smirks at her. "Later then. So hell yeah, baby, more drinks all round." Ev plants a longer than necessary kiss on her lips before slapping her ass as she saunters to the kitchen.

"Aren't they cute together, babe? I hope we're like that someday." Freya goes in for a kiss, but at the last second I turn my head just enough that her lips land on the side of my mouth. If I didn't need to keep up appearances in front of Everest, I would tell her *a-fucking-gain* that we're not like that. We're never going to be like that, she knows this. So I'm hoping this is all part of her ruse to make this whole marriage thing believable.

"I still need the bathroom though. I'll be back in a minute."

"Didn't River just go to the bathroom?" Freya's smile drops. *Fuck.*

"I don't know. I'll just wait outside the door if she did." *And make sure she's okay while I'm at it.*

"I'll come with you, then you don't have to wait on your own."

Her persistent need for us to be together is annoying the shit out of me, but I school my features. I may not like it, but I understand it. After all, I have been her one constant for the last few years. But again, nothing is as it seems.

"Freya, I'm a big boy. I can go to the bathroom by myself." I manage to untangle myself from her arms and start to walk away as Petal comes back in with freshly-filled glasses.

Finding out if River is okay shouldn't be a priority for me, but she's still my best friend. So actually, fuck it. I'm allowed to check in on her.

*That's what I'm trying to convince myself anyway.*

"Thanks, Petal. I was going to ask River if she wants to be my maid of honor. And I was hoping you'd agree to be a bridesmaid with my cousin? You and River are as close as family, so it feels right, you know?"

Shock stops me in my tracks. I'm sure I didn't just hear that right. River and Freya were best friends a long time ago, but I thought they'd grown apart. Freya continues talking wedding plans with Petal as I pause in the hall.

Can I handle having my Psyche, the other half of my soul, being a part of my wedding to someone else?

*What the fuck have I done?*

The bathroom door opens as I approach. River stands in the doorway, her face full of sadness. This can't just be about me and Freya. There's something else going on with my Psyche. It has to have something to do with that shit Ev brought up before Freya stole the limelight.

In two steps, I'm as close to River as I can get without touching her. If I do, all my resolve will crumble, and I can't humiliate Freya like that.

"What the fuck are you doing, Kai?" Her beautiful green eyes cut deep into my soul as she meets my gaze, backing up so her ass hits the counter in the bathroom.

"Tell me. What's going on with you? What fucked up shit happened?"

"You don't need to protect me. I'm a big girl, I can handle my own shit."

"Clearly not if you're running away to your brother's house."

Okay, so that probably—definitely—crossed the line if her expression is anything to go on. She's not hurt anymore, she's pissed.

"You're lucky you're my best friend or l would have to knock you on your ass for speaking to me like that. Your fiancé is in the other room, you really should fuck off back to her."

Her hands come up to push at my chest, to move me away from her. My Psyche might be a fierce and unstoppable warrior, but I'm her immovable object. Always here.

Reaching out, I grab her wrists with one hand, holding her chin with the other. I search out her eyes again, trying to read what she's not telling me, but her walls are impenetrable.

"River, drop the mask. Tell me what's going on. Please." The begging isn't something I'm used to, but desperate measures and all that shit.

"Ooh, please? That's almost a foreign word to you, isn't it?" She quirks a brow at me in challenge.

"River." My tone is hard and unyielding, and I hope it gets across how serious I am about this.

"Fine. I've got a stalker and whoever it is sent me a sick gift. All wrapped up with a pretty bow. I'm handling it, so you can go back to your fiancé and all the wedding planning."

"What the *fuck*?"

*Is she shitting me?* An anger like I've never felt before surges through me. I'm not even sure I'm thinking straight.

"I just need a few days out of the city and I'll be back to my old self again." The determination on her face says everything. She is not okay, but fuck if she ever tells anyone when she needs help.

"River, you've got a motherfucking stalker sending you things through the mail, and you think you're going to be okay after a few days? What is your boyfriend doing about it? Couldn't you stay with him?" The words feel like acid on my tongue, but if she were mine, I'd never let her out of my sight again. If I'm honest with myself, I never want to let her out of my sight anyway.

"Tyler and I broke up."

"What?" I hear her words but the meaning behind them takes longer than it should to reach my working brain.

She and the mogul are done?

As my eyes search her face for regret, the brief relief of her being available for me again allows me to take a deep, satisfying breath. How long has it been since I've actually reveled in the deep inhale of oxygen? Since the park, I realize. Since that day I confronted River in our old stomping grounds, facing the same fountain where, as a stupid kid, I'd told her I'd lost my virginity. In my defense, I was fifteen and horny and convinced myself that River didn't like me in that way since she'd friend-zoned me in the clearest of ways.

Just as soon as the warmth settles in my lungs, a two-hundred-pound rock drops in my stomach.

She ignores my outrage, rolling her beautiful eyes as she finally manages to move me away from her, walking out of the bathroom without even a backward glance.

What the actual fuck have I done?

I've fucked everything up because my ego got the better of me. I just wanted to give her space to grow, to become who she wants to be. She's always been mine, and I've always been hers.

But I gave myself away to someone else out of spite and pity.

My fucking ego needs a talking to.

# Chapter Two

## River

In any movie I've ever watched or novel I've ever read that was set in New York City, it was impossible not to consider it a character in and of itself. It's not just the majestic, imposing side of Manhattan; the borough that is known to practically seven billion people on Earth. It's also the proud and incomparable diversity of Queens, and although the Millennials' wet-dream, Brooklyn is still home to the most fascinating art scene in the country. It's the little-known history of The Bronx and the green haven of Staten Island's parks. It's the passion of New Yorkers when it comes to their food, music, or sports. It's the pride of announcing you're a New Yorker and not giving a fuck what other people think about your accent.

It's all of these things that make the Big Apple the most iconic city in the world.

But it's also suffocating. The constant noise and drones of people along the streets at any given time, day or night.

The vibrancy that creates life is also the very thing that makes lonely people feel even more invisible.

I rise to my heeled feet as the door to the bathroom opens and my new client crawls out. He's shackled at the wrists and ankles, barely able to make his way to me without faltering from lack of give.

"Stop." Stepping in front of him—my legs spread wide enough that my silk-covered pussy is just a few inches away from his face—I get into my regal stance and clasp my wrist behind my back, looking down at him like a dominatrix about to lash out for improper conduct.

The black suspenders, stockings, and matching silk bra all add to the general vibe I'm going for.

Elijah Duke kneels at my feet, his bound hands on his thighs and his head down in self-deprecating shame.

Our contract is a full ten pages of dos and don'ts, but as far as the person is concerned, I know very little.

What I've learned from my extensive background check is that he's ex-military but most of his files were classified and inaccessible, so beyond his rank and his honorable discharge, I don't have much to go on. He doesn't look a day older than his thirty-five years, but the weight of his pain has put an extra ten on his bearing; the slight slump of his shoulders, the defeated, methodical way he moves as if merely going through the motions.

He was referred by John, who comes to me once a year just so I can piss on his face before he disappears. When I spoke with him, he explained that post-traumatic stress was one of the big reasons his best friend, Elijah, was coming to me.

But maybe the most interesting tidbit I learned was his marital status. Not sure, yet, if they're still living together or maybe separated. It's all very hush hush for now.

Reaching out, I lightly tap the tip of my crop to the underside of his chin and guide his face up to mine, my features stern and devoid of emotion.

"Talk."

"Yes ma'am." I wait a beat then smack him on the cheek with my crop before repeating myself.

"I tried to fuck my wife but I can't get hard. *Fuck.*"

Here's the thing about Elijah Duke's contract. It outlines all of the things he wants me to do to him—the humiliation, the punishments, the degradation—basically getting his kink fix within the safety of my work studio.

"What punishment do you deserve for not being able to satisfy your wife?" Elijah bends at the waist and presses the side of his face onto the hardwood floor. Without uttering a single word, he tells me he deserves a whipping.

And I oblige.

In my line of sight, all I can see is an array of healing scars of all shapes and sizes across his back. His shoulders. His sides. I don't cringe because I'm a fucking professional, but my heart aches a little for him.

I start off soft, using a bat instead of a crop. The only difference between the two is the length. As I make my way around his side, I slide the flap over his head, down his neck and along his spine, until I reach the muscled globes of his tight ass. With three quick reps, I hum my satisfaction when a pink line begins to form.

Elijah doesn't utter a single word. He barely grunts.

Walking to the other side, I trail the bat along the way, repeating my three rapid strikes until a twin pink line joins the first. I'm not a domme, per se, but I have taken a few classes over the last couple of years. It's a fascinating art to learn and a great way to learn self-control, it's what I've needed most these past two weeks. Ever since the soul crushing news of Kai and Freya's engagement.

*And the motherfucking dick in a box.*

I suppress a shiver at the thought.

I haven't been back to Staten Island since the big announcement. Not because I don't want to see my brother and Petal—or even Kai—but because I need to take care of myself. I need distance to digest the news and what happened to me, and independently of all of that, I have a business to run; spending hours upon hours on a ferry instead of bringing in clients isn't very savvy.

Not allowing my mind to wander away from my job here, I refocus on my client.

"Why am I punishing you, Duke?" That's also in the contract. Calling him by his last name keeps the distance between us. Gives us a hierarchy where I'm at the top of the food chain and he's a mere mortal begging for forgiveness.

The only unknown variable is the why.

Why am I punishing him? Only he knows, and right now, he doesn't need me to play shrink with him. I'm guessing he has a real professional to help him with that. But again, it's none of my business.

"I can't fuck my wife." This time his words are stronger, less strangled, like his whipping is releasing some kind of guilt he has on his shoulders.

Without missing a beat, I switch up the implements, grabbing the longer crop to increase the pain of each slash.

Without waiting for long, I draw a series of pink to red lines across his ass cheeks, his lower back, his upper thighs.

"Do you want to come, Duke?" My voice is hard, stainless steel, just like he wants it.

"No, ma'am."

*Liar.*

Of course he does, but coming means betraying his wife and I don't think he wants to do that. This is his punishment for being so fucking kinky and not being able to talk to his wife about it. Of course, I'm guessing all of this since he hasn't actually talked about it with me, but it seems pretty elementary.

Jesus, now I sound like a kinky Sherlock.

I spend the next forty minutes painting his body with lashes of all sizes and intensities. My arm is sore from the exertion, my mind reeling from all the questions I have about his whys and hows. All I know is that he's the client and if he needs to talk, he will eventually.

And if he never does, well, at the end of the day, it's not my place to force him to speak. It's not what he pays me to do. It's not in the contract.

What is clearly written in black and white is that I must never touch him directly skin-on-skin. This client isn't about fucking, our sessions are about discretion and a safe space to degrade himself, to punish himself.

When we finish, I unhook him from his shackles—careful not to touch his skin—watching as the fire in his eyes comes back, increment by small increment.

I sit in the chair in the corner of my work studio, observing his every move. My instincts tell me war has a big part to play in the demons that haunt him, but that's a half-assed assessment about something I clearly don't understand.

"Everything okay?" I stand, my four-inch heels giving me the height I need to take up more space in a room where a bulky Marine could very easily overcome me. I'm not afraid of him but I'm not taking any more chances, either.

Naïve Rose disappeared the night a square patch of her skin was peeled off by a fucking psycho. I suppress another shiver at the thought of that night—the night a client got through Polly's background check and attacked me. Even though I escaped with my life, still, I lost a piece of myself.

"Yeah." Elijah buckles up his belt and barely spares me a look as he bends to tie his rangers. He's everything you expect a well-trained military officer to look like. Sharp, omni aware of his surroundings. Quiet and brooding. Handsome is an understatement and his scars don't take anything away from him. In fact, they make him seem real, like his flaws enhance his beauty. Cropped blond hair that matches his deep blue eyes with a smile that could make women feel like they're the only person who exists in the world.

Yet, I have a feeling he only uses that smile on one person.

His wife.

And that's why he suffers. He loves her, he wants her, but his kink—and I'm guessing his past—are ruining his normal.

That's what I'm here for, I suppose.

"I really appreciate your professionalism, Rose." He looks around like this entire conversation is making him uncomfortable.

"It's why I get paid the big bucks." The levity in my voice is exactly what he needs to release a tiny ounce of stress from his shoulders.

"Right. Well, I'll just..." He hooks a thumb over his shoulder and backs away, unsure of how to end this interlude.

"It's all good, Elijah. It's not a date. Just like a doctor's visit, say goodbye and walk out." I smile, trying to reassure him, and I'm relieved when it works.

With a self-deprecating chuckle, he nods and quietly walks out of my apartment.

I'm left alone and wondering—not for the first time—what the fuck happened to him to make him hurt so much.

# Chapter Three

## River

One of the perks of my profession—alongside the money and orgasms—is being able to choose my working hours. I'm not tied to the hustle and bustle like the average working American. It's been over a month since one of the worst experiences of my life to date, and while I've thrown myself into my job, I haven't been utilizing my downtime properly.

Admittedly, a dick in a box and Kai's surprise engagement didn't help. And though it's only been a couple weeks since then, it feels like a lifetime.

Yesterday was spent researching the best self-defense classes in Manhattan. My hope is that it gives me some of my power back. Putting on an act for my clients is one thing, but I need to feel safe in my own skin—and apartments. Making plans that don't involve clients has been therapeutic in a way. Plus, it's a great way to keep in shape.

Today, I'm putting my bad bitch panties back on and I'm going shopping. The majority of my money goes on necessities, Everest, or work things, but every now and then a little splurge on myself keeps me going. Plus, I need to get something to send Petal for her birthday in a few days. Dressed in my waist-high skinny jeans, fashionably torn, and my cream turtle-neck sweater, I sweep the long strands of my hair over to one side before applying my Velvet Teddy MAC lipstick. Paired with my trusty heeled Timbs and a jean jacket, I'm ready to go.

Mr. Bobby is on the stoop as I leave the building, in his usual spot, coffee in hand, watching the world go by.

"Morning, Mr. Bobby."

He looks up and holds his arm out, encouraging me to sit by him.

"Good morning, my girl."

His smile is infectious, the crinkle in his eyes only enhancing his sparkle.

"See anything interesting this morning?"

Sitting next to him, I rest my head on his shoulder as he puts an arm around me.

"We've had the usual Tuesday crowd so far, nothing too exciting. It's early yet, the day can still surprise me. You off to anywhere nice today?" He takes a sip of his coffee as he gently pats my arm, holding me against him like my dad used to.

"I'm on my way to Hudson Yards today. Figured the half hour it takes to get there will warm me up for all the shopping I'm planning to do."

His laugh rolls through me and fills me with the same joy it always does.

"Good girl. Be safe though, grab a cab on your way home if it gets late."

"Yes, Mr. Bobby. Don't worry." I go to stand, but he holds me to him for a moment longer.

"I'm glad to see some of your old spark back, I hate seeing my girl down and out. But if you gotta talk, I'm here, and that's all I'm saying on the matter. Now go." He kisses the top of my head in the same way I do to him.

It almost brings a tear to my eye. A little kindness goes a long way and he means well. I can't deny the sincerity in his voice. Mr. Bobby is a real contender for the kindest man in the world, alongside Santa.

The walk to Hudson Yards is relatively peaceful. Usually, I'd put my earphones in and strut my way there, but today I'm being more cautious. Paying attention to my surroundings.

Anyone would think I'm paranoid.

It doesn't stop me from scrolling through my phone as I walk though. I've exchanged a few messages with Ev, Petal, and even Kai over the last few weeks. Nothing exciting, the usual meme and joke sharing shit, where one of us sends something we think the others will find hilarious. The last one Ev sent in the group chat makes me laugh as I read it again.

**Ev:** Why didn't the lifeguard rescue the hippy?

**Kai:** Was he stoned?

**Petal:** The lifeguard or the hippy?

**Kai:** Both!

**Ev:** Because he was too far out, man.

**Me:** *cry-laugh emoji*

My phone pings with a new message, and I smile as I see who it's from.

**CAG:** Sooo... How long is a respectable amount of time between dates? Because I feel like I've waited too long. *see-no-evil monkey emoji*

He's messaged me a few times since our dinner together, but he works in a busy healthcare practice and hasn't had a lot of time to meet up again. It's usually late at night or after we've bumped into each other at the grocery store when we text. I won't lie and say I didn't wish Kai had been one of those late-night texts, but that's not going to happen. I put myself into a vulnerable position by believing I could do something about our relationship, and I was wrong. Lesson learned.

**Me:** I didn't realize we'd had any dates. *Laugh emoji*

**CAG:** Well, damn. I guess I must not have done it right. Does that mean we're just friends?

**Me:** *Shrug emoji* I guess we are.

His messages have put a spring in my step as I near the shopping center. I know my grin is cheesy as fuck, but I can't bring myself to give a shit. We've talked about our 'date' and being 'just friends', and I know our texts are just flirty fun. That's exactly what I need though; a little slice of normalcy away from all the expectations and heartbreak.

**CAG:** Well then, friend. I've got two tickets to the NY Knicks tomorrow night. You need to come with me so I'm not lonely.

**Me:** I'm sure there will be plenty of people for you to make friends with. You don't need little ole me.

I'm just playing coy now. Of course I want to go with him. I've lived in New York City my entire life and I've never been to a real life basketball game. I'm more of a baseball girl myself, so this should be fun.

**CAG:** Don't need you, no. I want you. Friend. Tomorrow night. I'll meet you at your apartment at 5:30pm.

**Me:** I didn't realize you were such a bossy one.

**CAG:** *winky face emoji* There are many things you don't know about me. So you better come.

**Me:** Friends don't make friends come. *Shock face*

**CAG:** I didn't peg you for a rule follower.

Well, he hasn't pegged me at all, but whatever.

**Me:** I guess there are many things you don't know about me either… See you tomorrow.

**CAG:** Tomorrow. 5:30pm.

Looks like I need to find a basketball game-worthy outfit while I'm here, and I'm actually excited at the prospect.

The hairs on the back of my neck prickle as I round the last corner to Hudson Yards, the huge imposing 'Vessel' looming in front of me. It looks like a giant work of art, the never-ending staircases in all directions, never actually leading anywhere. The paranoid feeling of being followed has been with me since I left my apartment, but as I near the mall entrance, it intensifies. I'm putting it down to the sheer amount of people walking around, but I'm not stupid enough to ignore it completely. Digging my keys out of my bag, I hold them in my palm, with the keys sticking out between my fingers. Better to be prepared than in a ditch.

I'll get a cab home when I'm finished here.

Dressed in my boyfriend jeans, a New York Knicks hoodie, and a team cap, I slide on my trusty Timbs, grab my crossbody bag and lock my apartment door behind me. Nathaniel has been outside talking to Mr. Bobby for the last ten minutes. I may or may not have been eavesdropping, but who could blame me? The way his Superman-style body fills out his own Knicks hoodie makes my clit tingle.

"You boys about finished down here?" Smiling at Mr. Bobby and Nathaniel as I exit the building, their conversation immediately stops. They both look up at me with equal grins on their faces. I swear, if this were a film, Nate's eyes and teeth would sparkle.

"You make sure you bring her home safe, young man. Ya hear?"

"Yes, sir." Nathaniel salutes Mr. Bobby before holding out his elbow for me to take, and I about melt at how fucking sweet this all is. "Ready to go?"

"I am. Don't stay out here all night waiting, Mr. Bobby."

He laughs and shakes his head. "Have fun, my girl."

Taking Nathaniel's outstretched arm, I wave goodbye to Mr. Bobby and we begin the short walk to Madison Square Garden.

"You're into the Knicks then?"

"Actually, no. But I wanted to look the part." I allow a small smile to play on my lips as he quirks a brow at me.

"Have you never been to a basketball game before?"

"Nope." Popping the P—which is practically the law when saying nope—I laugh at his mock-shock expression.

"I've got a lot to live up to this evening then. Okay, one full basketball game experience, coming right up!" The determination on his face makes me smile more as we join the crowds heading into the arena.

"You sure do, *friend*."

Well apparently, a full basketball experience involves stale beer and zero leg room. But I don't hate it, the atmosphere is infectious and the passion is palpable. Our seats aren't fancy, but our view is perfect. We are mid-court, among the Knicks fans, and I try to take it all in. The smiles and laughter, the matching hoodies and baseball caps, there are even a few orange and blue painted faces and huge foam fingers.

"What happened? Why is everyone cheering?" I was so busy taking everything in that I missed whatever was happening down on the court. Hell, the game hasn't even started yet.

Nathaniel looks out over the stadium and grins, the glint in his eyes making him appear younger than his age.

Wait, how old is he, anyway?

"That kid just got his shot. Bet he'll remember that for the rest of his life." Confused, I straighten my spine and follow Nathaniel's gaze, realizing it's the pre-game activities. When my eyes dart back to Nathaniel, I'm surprised to see a wistful cloud mar his normally open and happy features.

"Everything okay?" I'm not even sure he can hear me over the music.

"Yeah, of course." He glances at me, deep blue eyes swallowing me whole with their sincere depths. "Pre-game shoots for the kids are always great to see. These guys are idols for those children, and breathing in the same oxygen as them is a privilege they'll only fully appreciate later on in life." With a shrug, he raises a brow. "To show you how devoted I am to our friendship, I'm about to brave the pre-game lines. Beer or beer?"

"Oh the choices. I guess I'll go with... beer."

"Well, since we're going for the full experience here, you also have the choice between large or larg*er*. I'll even throw in a Top Dog and fries, and you can choose your toppings."

"You spoil me." I place my hands under my chin, giving him a head tilt and an Audrey Hepburn smile. "As if it's even a real decision. Larger. Always larger. And anything other than standard mustard is a travesty."

"You wound me. No onions? Sauerkraut? Spicy brown mustard?"

I laugh as he holds a hand to his heart in mock-horror. Shaking his head slowly as I raise a brow at him, he stands, backs away into the aisle, and disappears with a sly grin.

Twenty minutes in, the players are back on the sidelines and the wooden floor is getting a quick and thorough sweep when I feel a hand on my shoulder and jump like an electric shock has traveled through my spine. Gasping, I turn to see Nathaniel standing there in all his Superman*ish* glory—rolled up sleeves and arm porn included—handing me a simple mustard hotdog. His, on the other hand, looks disgusting.

"Don't judge me, Skittles. I'm a true New Yorker, not a mustard-only wannabe."

I make a fake gag move that only makes him laugh as he takes a seat and gives me my plastic beer cup. Good thing

I don't count calories or else this shit would be my worst nightmare.

"You truly are something else, River Fox."

I shrug.

Jesus, this man could make a nun's ovaries come out to play.

"And don't you forget it, Nathaniel Reed."

It's nearing the end of the game, and I don't know what I expected, but screaming for two and a half hours for a basketball team, wasn't it. My throat is raw and my cheeks ache. Throughout the game, I have been acutely aware of Nathaniel's every move. His lingering glances, his feathered touch against my arm, the brushing of our fingers, but what really does my head in is the whispered jokes in my ear. This man is a whole bag of nerdy rolled into a super sexy package.

It occurs to me in this moment that fucking him would not be the worst thing in the world. In fact, this whole friendship thing is complete and utter bullshit. And we both know it.

The reality of the situation seeps back in, destroying my fantasy. Friends is all I can offer, so friends it is.

The game finishes, and of course the Knicks have won. The crowd around us is going crazy celebrating, jumping out of their seats, arms in the air. Turning to Nathaniel, his bright blue eyes are watching me, a beaming smile on his face as I jump up and down like everyone around us. He raises his own arms, and brings me in for a hug, squeezing as he lifts me into the air.

A feeling of freedom washes over me as I settle in his hold, both of us whooping and hollering about being winners. As he puts me down, oh so slowly, my chest rubbing against his, I have to look up again to see his face. He doesn't move his arms from around my waist as he looks down into my eyes. The moment suddenly feels impossibly intense, my breathing becomes heavy and my nipples rub against his rock-hard body as I inhale and exhale like I've just run a marathon. Pretty sure Mr. Candy Aisle Guy is rocking a hard-on right now too, if the feeling against my stomach is anything to go by.

"Walk you home?" He breaks the building tension between us, and I'm grateful for the reprieve.

"You sure this isn't a date, friend?"

Holding out his arm, he tilts his head in the direction of the exit with a small smile. "Come on then. It's past my bedtime."

Hooking my arm around his, I gasp. "I knew it. You're an old man!"

His deep chuckle vibrates through my arm right to my core. "I'm only thirty-four, River. But keep up that sass and I'll show you just how old I'm not."

Oh damn, the sexy part of this nerd just got sexier.

Back outside my apartment, I feel like a teenager waiting for her first kiss, except I kind of want him to just grab me by the back of the head and feast on my mouth.

Yes, I know I already pulled away once, I know I'm not ready for anything serious, but that doesn't stop my traitorous body from wanting all the things.

"Thanks for a great evening, friend. Wanna do it again sometime?"

"Well, basketball is great and all, but I think next time I should teach you a thing or two about baseball."

He raises his brows at my statement, his lips tilted up in a perfect curve.

"Your honesty is like a breath of fresh air. Okay, we can do baseball. But I'm not waiting until baseball season starts next year to ask you out again."

"Ask me out? Like a date? Well that escalated quickly."

"Fuck it."

The next thing I know, his index finger hooks around my belt loop and my body is flush against the hard wall of his chest. We're both breathing hard, the expectation game so much more thrilling than any three pointer I witnessed on the court tonight. Bringing our foreheads together, he whispers, "You make me crazy, River."

I gasp at the sincerity in his voice and with a slight tilt of my chin, I give him my non-verbal yes. That's when his lips crash against mine, our breaths caught by the intensity of the moment, our mouths searching for more, for anything that could explain the chemistry we've felt buzzing all night. Hell, it's been there since the first time I met him between the Skittles and the Nerds.

"Nathaniel." His name comes out in a long exhale, all soft consonants and lust-ridden vowels.

With his lips still lingering against mine, his tongue licking at the seam, he traps my bottom lip between his teeth before leaving me panting and needy.

"Good night, Skittles." With one last stroke of his thumb against my chin, he backs away, his eyes never leaving mine.

They say everything his voice won't.

*I know you felt that.*

*I can't wait to do it again.*

*Next time, we won't be able to stop.*

Then with a final wave in my direction, he turns and walks away.

The front door is open as I approach, I'm pretty sure the latch is broken. Under normal circumstances, I'd report it and not think about it again, but after my delivery a couple of weeks ago, my mind instantly goes to all the shitty scenarios.

*Fuck.*

My insides start bubbling, and not in the fun '*I'm having a great time*' kind of way, more in the '*why won't my fears fuck off*' kind of way. Okay, I can do this. I can step inside.

*I'm a bad bitch and I own my shit.*

I will not allow other people to affect me in this way. I can't or I'd go fucking insane.

With a deep breath, or five, I finally step inside the building, taking my time to go up the stairs to my apartment. I take one step at a time, my back against the wall, and my eyes darting in every direction.

Times like this, I could really use my best friend. I'm not a damsel who needs saving and can't look after herself, but shitty things have happened, and I just feel safer with him around. More confident.

It's fucking stupid, but that's just how it is.

He's always been my safe space, but now it's time to create a new one.

There's nothing untoward as I slowly approach my apartment door and I feel myself relaxing slightly as I unlock it and step inside. The breath I didn't realize I'd been holding finally releases as I close the door behind me—locking the three bolts— and switch on all the lights I possibly can.

My evening has been ruined by these annoying niggles, and my butterflies have disappeared. I'm going to have to get those self-defense classes booked as soon as possible. Having the confidence to protect myself is a priority.

Fuck this paranoia shit.

# Chapter Four

## River

I've decided I'm not a fan of the full-body pleather get-up. Do I look sexy as fuck in it? Absolutely. Would I wear it all day long? Not even Tyler Walker's payday could make me do it.

The thought brings a pang to my chest.

I wonder, not for the first time, how he's doing. I've read Page Six a couple of times in hopes of seeing him, making sure he's okay. I suppose I could call him but I don't want to give him any false hope.

Or maybe I just don't want to complicate my life any more than it already is.

Shaking away all thoughts of Tyler, I take the three steps I need to make it to Elijah, who is tied to the St. Andrew's cross I had to buy for this occasion—silent. Well, he had to buy it since it was his request to have one.

It cost a pretty penny, too, but it looks at home in my studio. Thank fuck I don't host dinner parties here. Well, unless someone is feasting in my pussy, that is.

"Are you comfortable?" My question is almost rhetorical since comfort isn't something Elijah particularly wants.

He needs pain. Craves degradation. The bondage being too tight won't make him squirm, but it's my duty to make sure he's safe, even if he's not capable of making that decision himself.

A barely audible grunt is what I get.

"Use words." I accentuate each syllable with a small slap of my crop to his cheek.

"Yes ma'am."

"Good." He doesn't get off on the compliments or positive reinforcement. Like I said, he just needs the pain, which is what I give him.

I'm dressed in red to match the cross. Only my accessories are in black and it all feels quite choreographed.

"How are last week's lashes healing?" I'm asking to see if he answers honestly. I've seen the welts and they are barely-there scabs now, a week later.

"Good. Kept them clean with antibacterial cream."

Great answer. It means he's taking care of himself. So why does he look like he's carrying the weight of the entire world on his shoulders?

"Should we talk before I begin? Anything I need to know?" I give him time to respond. Talking about feelings and shit isn't always an easy thing to do.

After a while, he shakes his head as he verbally tells me he's ready to go.

And so it begins.

The teasing, the caressing, the quick hits to the front of his thighs. Unlike last time, he's not getting hard. His eyes aren't glazing over with his endorphins. If anything, he's not even enjoying it. At all.

I stop everything and wait for him to realize I'm not continuing.

"Corpus Christie."

*Well, shit.*

Elijah Duke just safe-worded, and we've barely even begun.

As per the rules, I drop the crop and immediately untie him from the cross, making sure to never touch him skin-on-skin.

Neither of us speaks as he walks into the bathroom and does whatever he needs to do. I take the time to quickly change into something less dominatrix and more college-student-about-to-take-finals, before heading for the small kitchen and pulling two water bottles out of my nearly empty fridge. I leave the dark brown wig on, tied at my nape, it's comfortable and light. Besides, I've only ever taken it off for one client and that was Tyler. The man exudes exceptions. His very essence says he's not all men. He's above it all. So he got to fuck me with his fingers clenched around my short strands.

Elijah Duke is no Tyler Walker. He is a slave to his kink but above all, he's in love with his wife.

Fifteen minutes later, he walks out dressed in the clothes he arrived in—dark jeans and a Henley.

"You okay? Have some water, Elijah." I hold out the bottle and give him my "don't fuck with me" eyebrow arch.

"Yeah, sorry about that." Sliding onto the stool, he rests his corded forearms onto the breakfast island and looks up at me through his long-as-fuck lashes.

Why are all the men in my life so fucking hot? Okay, totally inappropriate, but still, the question begs to be asked.

"Never apologize for using a safe word. It's why they're there." I shrug and take a sip of my water, my gaze never leaving him. Fuck, that pleather shit made my body temperature rise by thirty degrees.

"Right, you're right but..." Taking a sip of his water, he lets his words linger and at this point, I'm convinced the conversation has stopped there. "I got served today."

"Served? Like, you're being sued?" You always see that shit on television but I have never met someone who's actually been served. I imagine some random dude walking up to him and asking his name before saying the famous words and running away.

"Divorce."

And everything clicks into place.

*Fuck.*

"Oh. I'm sorry to hear that. Were you not expecting it?" This is so none of my business, but curiosity and all that shit.

"I don't know, really. We're separated, but fuck... we talked about couples therapy just last week. But then I told her I was getting some help and mentioned you..." He looks up at me and I'm not sure what he was expecting. Anger? Fear? He gets none of those things because this is not my first rodeo. I know how to handle the crazy that comes with the territory. "I'm sorry."

"No need to be. This is your dime, Elijah. You get to decide who knows what. You get to share your kinks, you know? How did she take it?"

He cocks a brow as if he's waiting for my brain to catch up with the conversation. Divorce, right.

"Ouch." I nod slowly, taking another sip when an idea forms in my head. But first, I have questions.

"Does she know about your need for pain?" I'm standing on the other side of the kitchen counter, right across from him, so I'm taking in all his cues, his tells, his little mouth twitches and brow furrows.

"Yeah, she freaked out for a minute but then started asking all these questions about what I liked and I just... I don't know. It was awkward. The idea of her seeing me bound to a cross makes me want to throw up."

"Why?" I'm truly confused now.

"Because I'm a man, Rose. I don't want her to see me as anything but strong and, it's going to sound stupid but—an alpha." I'd laugh if it wasn't so heartbreaking. I don't answer right away, I let him digest his own words before gently placing my bottle on the counter and boring my gaze into his.

"Hmm, so handing over the reins to your wife takes away from your alphaness?" Pretty sure that's not a word but it doesn't matter at this point.

Elijah lets the question bounce around his head for a while. I can see his brow crease, his lips curling up and down as he thinks about it all. Finally, he looks back up at me and with sincerity oozing from every word, he finally answers.

"I suppose not."

"She asked to help you and you refused her. You told her no when she showed interest in sharing your kinks. But then you tell her you've hired some chick to do it for her? I'm betting all of this has something to do with pride and hurt." It seems so logical to me but from the lightbulb moment that is visible in Elijah's eyes, it obviously wasn't so apparent for him.

"Holy fuck, Rose." It's all he says as he finishes off his bottle of water.

"You know what? Ask her to come here with you. Bring her into your world for our next appointment. Be open with her, show her you trust her with your well-being. At this point, the worst she can do is serve you divorce papers. Oh wait..." I shrug, the attempt at humor taking a second. "Too soon?"

And for the first time since I've known him, Elijah's gorgeous face breaks out into a real charm-the-panties-off-all-the-ladies grin that must have gotten him laid a million times over the years.

My job here is done.

There's a spring in my step as I walk back to Kips Bay from my work studio. It's days like this where I don't feel so bad for letting my family believe I'm a life coach. Because, right now, I feel like one.

My apartment is only five minutes away, but it's getting late; the sun has just set, and I'm not a dumb bitch. I have my keys in hand, poking out between my fingers as my only form of defense right now. Not that I've ever needed it in all my years of living here, but the paranoia is real. I should probably see a shrink about it at some point, but it's not top of my priority list. I'm handling my shit.

The sound of Halestorm hits my ears, pulling me away from my surroundings on East 27th. It's a busy street, full of skyscrapers and beautiful architecture, and because of its higher-class reputation, it feels relatively safe.

Checking my phone, I see it's Kai calling. We've spoken briefly via text since the announcement, but nothing of any substance. I won't deny I miss him, the late night calls we'd share talking about everything and nothing, sometimes just sitting in silence as we watched *Lucifer* with each other on speaker phone. All the best friend stuff.

Steeling my spine, I answer the call. He must be calling for a reason, and even though I'm mad at him, he's still my best friend. All that doesn't go away with a few shitty decisions—on both our parts.

"Hey Kai. What's up?"

Nothing.

For fuck's sake, this just takes me back to the weird-ass phone calls that conveniently stopped after my dick gift arrived. Anxiety seems to be growing a new home inside me as it rears its ugly head. Taking a deep breath, I look down at my cell, it's showing a missed call. Which actually sends a flood of relief through me. This anxiety bullshit is pissing me off. One minute I'm paranoid, the next I'm almost drooping with relief.

I am now wondering why Kai called though. But it can wait, I'll get back to him once I'm home. If it's urgent, he'll try again or send a message.

In some ways, Kai is very similar to Elijah. They both project a very intense alpha-male energy, when in reality, they have layers. Lots and lots of layers. I couldn't begin to define Elijah's, but Kai's? Well, I'd be able to write a novel about his. Not that I understand them all, because I really don't. It's a whole communication thing, another similarity to Elijah. Neither of them can properly communicate what they want.

Turning the corner off East 27th onto Lexington, I'm mere minutes away from my apartment. But that's when the horrible feeling of being watched comes back. For the last few months, it's been coming and going. With the psycho incident, it increased tenfold. Though I put the increase down to being paranoid after suffering through a traumatic event. The dick in a box just made the feeling skyrocket, and I've been paying attention to my inner fear ever since. Not that it's done anything for me other than make me more anxious.

I'm not stopping to look around, that's what the dumb cunts in films do right before they get stabbed—that, or they run up the stairs. Luckily, there are no stairs for me to contend with. Instead, I keep my eyes forward and chastise myself for losing focus on my surroundings. It's not so busy on this end of town, but there are still cabs and other vehicles flying by and lighting up the street as they pass.

A scream escapes my throat as I'm pulled back by my short hair, the smell of nicotine hitting my nostrils as a giant hand covers my nose and mouth. I can't fucking breathe.

My feet bang against the ground as I'm dragged along the street and into a gated alleyway.

"Shut the fuck up." The deep growl of a Brooklyn accent is in my ear as his hold tightens and brings that anxious ball right back into my stomach. It expands to my legs, my arms, my heart, and I can feel tears of anger and fear prickling at my eyes as I struggle to get away.

The sidewalk soon cuts off, and my feet are now scraping along a dirt track as I struggle to get out of his hold. The bracket lamp on the wall at the entrance of the alley moves further away, and the noise of the street quiets. His shallow breaths and footsteps mixed with a horrible menthol smell are filling my senses.

Stopping, he looks around before thrusting me against the wall cheek first. One hand covering my mouth, the other holding a knife I didn't see until now up against my ribs. He moves closer as the brick wall scratches at my face, where I'm sure a bruise is already forming on my cheek.

His erect crotch connects with my lower back, and he starts to rub himself against me.

*No, no, no, no, no!*

This isn't fucking happening. My hands are empty, I dropped my keys and phone at some point. Fat load of good holding my keys for protection did.

It's not easy with his hold so tight, but I manage to open my mouth, my muffled screams getting me nowhere. Not that I'm stopping. Biting down, I try real hard not to taste him, rolling my tongue back as far as it can comfortably go.

"Argh! You fucking whore!"

A sharp pain digs into my ribs, and I immediately stop screaming. His hand may be gone from my mouth, but I don't want to die today. I don't imagine being stabbed is a fun way to go. My head is again smashed into the brick wall, causing the wound already on my cheek to throb even more as a stinging sensation above my eye shoots through me.

"You ungrateful whore. Aren't you going to thank me for your gift?"

It was him? The only gift I've received is... yeah... well. Sick fuck. It takes everything I have inside me not to puke. He starts rubbing himself against me again, his hand back on my mouth.

I'm frozen. For the second time in as many months, I'm in a situation I never thought I'd be in. When—not if—I make it out of this, I need to do something more, something proactive to protect myself. Adrenaline is flooding my body and I'm shivering, trying real hard to control my shaky breaths and not give this sick bastard anything to get off on.

"Why did you go to the police? Huh? Didn't I tell you to be fucking careful?"

His nose hits my neck, and he takes a long, deep inhale. It sends a shiver of disgust rolling through me, the tears streaming down my cheeks now.

"Mmm. You smell fucking divine for—"

"Hey! What's going on down there?" A deep, rumbling voice interrupts my attacker's advances.

"Fuck. I'm coming for you, my little whore. Soon."

Oh my good fucking God. I sag to the ground as he releases me, and relief like I've never felt before flows through my body, finally allowing my angry sobs to escape as I hold my arms around myself.

"Hey! What's going on down there?"

The voice is different from the first one, and as I look up through my tear-filled eyes, I can see four men and a woman heading in my direction. One of them has the flashlight of their phone on to see better, and as it shines on me he starts running.

"Holy shit, are you okay?" He crouches down in front of me, the others joining him quickly as I square my shoulders and take a deep breath. I won't break in front of people.

"We heard a phone ringing by the entrance then noticed you down here. What a fucking scumbag. Are you okay? Can you move? Do you want us to call anyone?"

The woman's attitude takes me aback for a second, but damn, I think I like her, she has an amazingly strong aura. The four guys form the perfect half circle around her, like her own little harem.

"Thank you. So much." I'm struggling to find words, but the more I speak, the more I can feel my strength coming back. My trusty mask slipping into place. I don't want to be River right now. "Honestly, thank you. The fucker's gone now, but I can't tell you how grateful I am."

Pushing against the wall, I stand, and the five of them stand with me. I should feel intimidated by them, but I don't. My instinct is usually right with people. Psycho stalker guy gave off some bad juju that constantly made me want to throw up, these guys give off more of a protective vibe.

"Holy shit, your face! Sorry, that was rude, you're bleeding." The concern in the woman's eyes is evident as she reaches up to push my hair from my face.

"You might want some stitches."

"Is it bad, Ash?" The girl addresses the nerdy-looking guy covered in ink, and he frowns at her, shaking his head before moving away from me. After addressing him, she turns back to me. "He's right though, that looks nasty. Can we help?"

"I just need to find my keys and phone so I can get home. I've got a first-aid kit." Rubbing my hand across my forehead, I wince as my fingers brush against my eyebrow. That's bleeding then.

"Are these yours?" The twin to the nerdy one, who radiates a golden retriever energy, holds up my phone and keys, like a freaking angel in disguise.

"Yes! Oh my God! Where did you find them?" Taking them from him, I hold them close, placing my keys between my fingers, which is fucking pointless now. I'm feeling a little stronger—even though it's an act I'm allowing my body to play out—and not having lost these things is a win. And I fucking need that right now.

"The keys were a few feet from the ringing phone that caught our attention. Good thing it did and that we aren't the kind of assholes who'd just walk on by."

*Kai.*

I know it was him. I can just feel it in my bones.

The thought soothes my warring mind, but this is neither the time nor the place for this. I push the thoughts aside to deal with when I get home.

"Thank you, guys. Really." I move to start walking, and they all follow.

"Do you want us to walk you back to your apartment?" The bulky, dark, brooding one to my right surprises me with his deep voice, and under other circumstances this could be a total clit-tingling moment. But it's not, and I get the feeling the girl would punch me in the tit if I said anything.

"No. I'm good. It's only two minutes from here. I want to stop at the store on the way before it closes."

We're here, at the alley entrance. Fucking Broadway Alley. Forever ingrained in my mind.

"Are you sure? We don't mind, we've got time." The girl moves to put her hand on my arm, causing me to wince at the near contact. "Sorry, I didn't mean..."

"It's fine." It's not, but it's also not her problem.

"Do you want to take my number for the police report?" She's pulling her phone out before I can answer.

I'm not going to the police this time. I can't.

That is definitely one of those stupid thoughts people have when they think they can take care of shit themselves, but fuck it. The police have done fuck all so far. I haven't heard anything from them since the report a few weeks back. Not to mention, this whole thing would bring about an investigation. What if they find out about my two apartments? No life coach can afford that. And maybe they'll want to search it out. I can't have those kinds of eyes on me.

I just can't.

Like a blanket of darkness, the numbness about the whole situation seeps through my veins.

"Sure. Here's my card. Send me a text with your details and I'm sure they'll be in touch once I've reported it." I know I'm being a little colder with her than I need to be, considering they just stopped fuck knows what from happening to me, but I just need to move. To be among the familiar, to top up my wine supply. Fuck, tonight might even be a whiskey night.

"Are you sure you're okay?" Her voice reminds of my mother's when I'd scrape my knee; firm yet warm.

"Just a little shaken up. But I'll be fine, I promise."

With an awkward wave, I thank them again, ignoring their scowls and piercing gazes as I turn to leave. They're worried, I get it, but at this very moment, I just need to get the fuck out of here.

It all quickly blurs into nothingness as I allow what happened to replay in my brain, and almost on auto-pilot, I head toward the grocery store.

# Chapter Five
## Nathaniel

*Red wine or dark ale?*

I'm standing in the alcohol aisle of my favorite corner grocer and can't for the life of me make a goddamn decision. All day long, I'm quick on my feet juggling sometimes three patients at a time and delegating my needs and instructions to the nurses, but here, after hours, I'm incapable of deciding if I want something rich and fruity or cold and bitter.

"Red, white, yellow, blue..." I'm tired. Must be exhausted if I'm resorting to counting rhymes to choose my alcohol.

With a resigned sigh, I turn around and grab my usual box of pasta with the blue and white label and something written in Italian. I speak it a little. What born and bred New Yorker doesn't have essential words? *Stronzo, pasta, risotto, bella*.

Okay so "speak it" might be a stretch.

I've watched all the Godfathers' and Untouchables. The Goodfellas, and what was the one with DeNiro?

Right, he's in all of them at one point, isn't he?

Rubbing at the pain starting to pierce behind my temple—as it always does after work—I turn to grab whatever my hand touches first when a gasp and then a screech coming from Francesca, the owner of the shop, sends me on high alert.

"*Dio!* What happened?" The trained doctor in me has dropped the shopping basket and in five steps I'm at the front entrance, assessing the older lady first, and thirty seconds later, I'm staring into the bright green—albeit bloodshot—eyes of the woman who consumes my every thought.

"River?" Her name is a long breath of shock that escapes between my lips. With blood smeared over her face like she tried and failed to wipe it off, my gaze zeroes in on the nasty cut right above her eye, the skin flapping as it hangs over onto her eyelids.

*What the hell?*

Without touching her, I approach slowly. Her breathing is a series of hitched staccatos, her eyes darting from left to right but not settling on anything in particular. As I check out her other wounds—the scrape on her cheek needs to be cleaned or else she'll end up with an infection—I see her hands shaking as she clutches her phone and keys so tightly I'm afraid something will have to give.

"River." I repeat her name, hoping she'll break out of the shock she's trapped herself into.

"Should I call the police?" I nod to Francesca just as River's head snaps to the side and with a voice so strong and calm, I watch in awe and maybe a little fear, as the woman before me transforms from a confused and frightened doe to a strong and powerful lioness.

"No, thank you, Francesca. It's nothing. I fell." There isn't a single person in this shop who believes her. The other patrons are watching us, whispering and assessing just as I am.

"River..." I start to argue even though the look on her face tells me I need to shut my mouth. But I'm a doctor, and if she won't call the police, she has to—at the very least—allow me to clean her wounds and possibly get a stitch or two on her brow.

"Nathaniel, you're sweet for worrying but I just need to get a few things then go home." Her eyes speak louder than her words. It's the sheen threatening to spill over, the dilation of her pupils, the tightness in the skin around her eyes.

"Let me take you home and clean you up. You need stitches, River. Let me do this. Please." I hope she can see the same desperation in my stare as I do in hers.

"Okay. Fine."

"Good." I take out a handkerchief that I always carry in the inside pocket of my jacket—an old tradition my father instilled in me—and hand it to River. "For your eyebrow." I nod at the mess that is going to, no doubt, leave a scar.

It's when she raises her hand to take the square fabric from me that I see it.

"Fucking hell, River, you're bleeding." My eyes dart from her face to just below her ribs, where a patch of red has stained her white shirt enough to make alarm bells sound in my head.

"What?" With brows knitted and lips turned down, she raises her arms into the air to look at where I'm slowly pulling her shirt away. I need to know if it's a scratch or a deep laceration. Maybe I can just put on a dressing or a couple of sutures, because she can't just walk around bleeding like that.

Francesca comes up to me with my groceries and a few extra things—including a first-aid kit—and practically pushes us out the door.

"Go! Go take care of our girl." That woman is tiny, I could probably bench press her with one arm as I eat my spaghetti with the other, yet she's got enough strength to get me out the door with a big bag of shopping in tow.

I don't waste time, though. I make a mental note to go back tomorrow and pay for whatever it is that I'm taking with me.

Right now, my first and only priority is River.

When we reach her apartment, Mr. Bobby isn't on the stoop and I'm grateful. River is a proud woman and I'm guessing running into me has filled her humiliation quota by a mile.

"Keys?" My voice is calm and soothing, a low tone that doesn't catch her off guard.

"Yeah." River uncurls her fingers, her keys appearing in the palm of her hand. A hand that is covered in scrapes and a small, almost insignificant, cut that I'm guessing she caused with how hard she was clenching the metal between her fingers.

Cupping her wrist, I bring her palm to my lips and ever so lightly whisper a kiss on her wounds. She's lying. That's clear as day. Falling doesn't cause trauma, being attacked does. I know. I've seen it a hundred times.

"Let's get you inside and all better, okay?" She nods curtly, like this is no big deal, and I wonder why she feels she has to act so strong when obviously, she needs help.

I don't tell her this, of course. Instead, I'm the rock she needs as she leads the way to her apartment, and I realize I've never been inside. I am disappointed that it has to be under these circumstances.

The door closes behind me and I'm immediately in doctor mode. Taking off my leather jacket, I place it on the chair and unbutton my cuffs before rolling up the sleeves and securing them at my elbows.

"Bathroom?" I raise a brow at River, my question lingering for a brief moment before she shakes her head.

"Right behind you." I start for the door, but turn back to River and walk right over to her. Gently placing my hands on her neck where there are no wounds, I lean down and barely press my forehead to hers, whispering so my words are just for this little bubble I've created.

"You're okay. I'm going to clean you up, put you to bed, then make you a nice hot tea." *Then I'll fantasize about killing whoever did this to you.*

"I hate tea."

"Coffee, then." I smile, needing to bring her some lightness.

"Too late for coffee." The corners of her mouth tick up and it feels like an Olympic victory.

"Whiskey?"

"Perfect."

"Done. But only one sip, I don't need you bleeding out on me."

Sweeping her hair back, I drop a chaste kiss at her temple and pull her with me to the bathroom, bag in hand. Thankfully, her light is bright enough that I won't do a shit job on her cut.

Watching as River stares at the wall in front of her, eyes fixated on nothing in particular, I wash my hands, making sure to scrub between my fingers.

"Here's what's going to happen, Skittles." After rinsing, I add more soap and repeat my every move before elaborating.

"You're going to take a shower and when you're done, I'll clean up your wounds and inspect them before treating you. I'm most worried about the one on your eyebrow." I nod in her direction and her eyes slide to meet my gaze.

River doesn't move for the longest time and just when I think I'll have to resort to my doctorly voice, I hear her.

"Will you go in there with me?" To be honest, I'm not sure how to respond to this. Part of me wants to protect her, make her feel safe, but this isn't how things were supposed to happen and the responsible part of me refuses to take advantage of her.

"River..." I'm not sure if I'm shaking my head to deny her or to convince myself to stay rooted right where I am.

"Nathaniel, please. I don't want to be alone."

*Fuck. Fuck. Fuck.*

"River, I ca—"

"Please," she begs this time, with her words and her eyes.

I'm an asshole because I cannot refuse her. Hands on my hips, I hang my head and take a couple of fortifying breaths, giving myself a moment to come to my fucking senses.

And then she crosses her arms and pulls her white shirt up and over her head, leaving her in a black lace bra that makes her skin look flawless, despite the small cut by her rib.

"This is wrong, River. You're in shock and one of us has to keep a level head."

Her jeans drop next and I actually turn around to give her privacy. Pressing my palms to the door frame, I latch onto the wood as a last-ditch effort to stay put.

The sound of the glass door sliding open, coupled with the whoosh of the showerhead releasing the water, has me breathing even harder.

"You can stay dressed if you want, but you don't have any clothes here." *Fuck*.

I tell myself I'm doing this for River. The shower will not only clean her up but it'll soothe any inevitably sore muscles. I can't imagine she didn't try to fight her way out of whatever happened tonight.

I tell myself I'll be there in case she has a concussion and falls. I'll stay professional.

I tell myself all of these things and I believe them, except for one detail... she's River and I've thought about this for way too long.

The next thing I know, I'm in my boxer briefs and helping her step into the shower. I don't dare touch her anywhere but her hand as I make sure she's stable. Then I stand back and let her do her thing.

She strips off her bra and panties, obviously unbothered by her nakedness—killing me a little in the process—as she stands under the jet of the showerhead and lets the water rinse away the events of the night. The tension is visibly leaving her shoulders, the cords along her neck relaxing little by little, and for that, I'm grateful.

When her hand darts out to grab the shampoo, I act on instinct. On muscle memory.

I grab the bottle and take a step forward.

"Let me." The words are out before I can stop them and by the slight smile on her face, I've made her happy.

If nothing else, that counts for something.

Pushing out a dollop of cream onto my palm, I lather it up before gently coating her short hair with it, careful not to touch her face or hurt her in any way.

The little vixen moans. As if I'm not using my sheer will to keep my hands to myself, she makes the kind of noise I dream of hearing in my bed.

My eyes are focused on only her hair and face but I can't control my peripheral vision, and every drop that slides down her body makes me wish these were different circumstances.

Once I'm certain her hair is nice and clean, I guide her one step back so she can rinse it out.

She moans again and it's all I can do to keep my dick in my boxers. It's then she does the unthinkable.

As I'm gathering her short strands in a wet knot to wring out the last of the shampoo, River slides her fingers between mine and pulls my hand down her neck, her collarbone, her chest, before pushing up on her tippy toes and placing her mouth a mere inch away from my parted lips.

My breaths are shallow, my chest rising and falling with the effort to keep that inch between us. To keep myself from closing the distance and devouring her in all the ways possible.

River makes the decision for me, her hand at the back of my neck, her lips crashing against mine. I'm the one who moans this time as she slides her tongue inside my mouth and searches out my passion. She doesn't have to wait long. My control has all but evaporated as the pads of my fingers dig into her nape, pulling her impossibly closer.

We feast on one another. Devouring our pasts and regrets. Soothing our pains and giving each other hope with every brush of our tongues. There are no plans, no decisions to make. Only this moment and this kiss.

I'm hard, my cock straining to have more, do more, feel so much more.

Thankfully, I come to my senses and extricate myself from her hold.

"No, River. Not like this." Her eyes pop open and it's like she's seeing me for the first time. Without a single word, she turns back around and grabs her loofah and her flowery scented body wash before quickly lathering herself up and rinsing it all away.

In silence, we both step out of the shower and as I hand her a clean towel, she smiles up at me with gratitude.

Fuck, that was close.

"Will it leave a scar?" We're both in our towels as I survey the cut on her brow.

"Probably. I need to take a closer look to know more." Picking her up at the waist, I sit her on the counter before rummaging inside the bag and opening the first-aid kit. Francesca wasn't playing around with this one. It's complete with a suture kit and cyanoacrylate adhesives. Although, if my suspicions are correct, the cut is too jagged for me to use the medical glue.

Sliding on the latex gloves, I push the longer ends of her wet hair aside and place her hand there so she can hold it away for me.

"Make sure it doesn't fall in your face, okay?" My tone leaves no room for argument. I'm in healer mode and there's nothing more annoying than hair falling in a wound while you're working on it. "This is probably going to sting, but you're kind of a badass so I'm sure you'll be fine."

She snorts at this and it makes me smile on the outside, while on the inside I'm livid.

Going through the motions, I explain everything I'm doing, all the while keeping my eyes on her every move. The first-aid kit's sutures will be enough and thankfully, she'll only need three. It'll be swollen for a few days but it should heal nicely. What worries me most is that I have no idea if she's hit her head, if she has a concussion.

"If you'd tell me what happened, I could get a better idea of the level of treatment you need."

"I fell." I take a deep breath and barely hold myself back from calling her out on her lie.

"When I was an intern, we had an attending that was exceptionally hard on us. He never spoke unless it was absolutely necessary. Wasn't much for compliments either." I disinfect the area and am relieved to see that she doesn't start bleeding again.

Next, I peel the bottom corner of the towel away so I can work on the cut just below her ribs. It's not nearly as deep as I had feared.

But of course, because the universe wants to punish me for whatever reason, River takes it upon herself to drop the towel all together. I scowl up at her and she just shrugs like it's no big deal.

My cock begs to differ.

"That's the worst anecdote I've ever heard." Blinking back my confusion, I glance back up at her and frown.

"What?"

"Your story. It's like a hanging sentence or a cliffhanger in a Romance book." I grin up at her, relieved that the River I know is slowly coming back.

"Patience, little padawan. Intern anecdotes must be savored. There is always a moral to the story." Bringing my attention back to my work, I'm happy to see that it's superficial but the sight of it still pisses me off.

Who the fuck did this to her?

"Right. Well, I'm waiting with bated breath." There's almost humor in her tone, like she's trying to fight her way out of her trauma. That's okay, I'll pull her out by the sheer will of my feelings for her if she can't make it out on her own.

"Smartasses don't get the end of the story, you know. Usually, what happens during your first-year internship stays at the hospital. Fight Club rules apply." I'm making it up as I go along. Intern stories are created to be shared and laughed about years later because if you survive that first year, then you deserve the stories.

"I'm sure." She looks at me then, her light breaking through whatever darkness was snuffing it out. I'm like a dog with a bone, needing to know she's all right.

But I don't dare break whatever progress she's making. So I give the lady what she wants.

"Dr. Manchin was a hardass. I mean, he would call you out for chewing too loudly." She nods, probably knowing the type. "So, one night, I'm in the E.R. doing grunt work for the attendings when all hell breaks loose. The EMTs rush in through the sliding glass doors, rattling off the patient's stats. She was barely hanging on for life if her oxygen levels were any indication, but as an intern, I was expected to listen, watch, and keep my mouth shut unless asked to speak." I freeze as River gasps.

"You okay?" Looking up, my gaze does a quick assessment of her facial features. Brows pinched, skin tight around the eyes, top teeth biting down on her bottom lip. "Did I hurt you?"

River shakes her head and it's then I realize, while I'm cleaning and applying antibacterial cream on her cut, my free gloved hand is rubbing soothing circles on the bare skin of her thigh. I stop immediately, thinking we might be pushing the limits of our control, and in that same moment the overwhelming feeling of déjà-vu hits me from out of nowhere. I learned the hard way that, sometimes, all the degrees and training in the world can't save the ones we love. We can't save everyone.

*I* can't save everyone.

Not even Angelica. But that's a story for another time.

"Don't stop." Her voice brings me back to the situation at hand and I don't know if she means the story or the circles, so I continue both.

"It's when we rush over to the gurney that we come face to face with the reality of the situation. It's a little girl—eight, if I remember correctly—and she's practically naked her clothes are so impossibly torn. She's completely cut up, like some sick bastard was playing with his knife and she was his sculpture. She's alive but when Dr. Manchin leans in to shine the ophthalmoscope in her eyes; she barely reacts." I'm choked up at the memory. The feeling of helplessness in that moment when my oath means shit all because even if we physically heal her, mentally, she'll never be the same. Never. Something I know about all too well.

"She was in shock." River's voice is barely a whisper, but the strength in those four words is unmistakable.

"Yeah. Her mind was on full-duty protection mode." I clear my throat, the memory bringing with it all the emotions of that night.

"I'm in shock, too, Nathaniel." My name on her lips makes me pause. Fuck, I'm not supposed to love it so much.

"Yeah, you are, Skittles." Bringing her hand to my lips, I give her a light kiss, lingering there for a second longer than intended. "But you'll be okay. I promise."

"What happened to the girl?" The hope in her eyes is killing me.

"Her name was Lillybeth Summers." My voice cracks at the sound of her name. It's been so long since I've said the words. "Every despicable thing that could happen to a child, she endured. For days. She—"

"Her mind protected her to the end?" The lump in my throat grows to the size of an orange, and I fight back the familiar and inevitable burn behind my eyes any time her story comes up. Nevertheless, River needs to hear the whole thing.

"She refused to tell us what happened. Refused to speak or even make eye contact. She would nod or shake her head. Only once did we hear her voice, and it was when her father came running inside the E.R., wanting to take her back home. I've never seen social services move so quickly and efficiently." Placing the dressing on her skin, I use the tape to secure it and then back away to look at my handiwork, before passing her the towel which she wraps around herself. I need her covered for my own sanity.

"You'll need to keep the wound clean and try not to get it wet. That said, you should only need the dressing for forty-eight hours, max." River clutches my wrist and waits until I stop everything and look back at her.

"What happened to Lillybeth?" With a sigh, I gently make space between her legs before I cradle her head in the palms of my hands. River's looking at me with expectation in her eyes and hope in her depths. There's only a towel separating her smooth skin from my bare body and the thought is sobering.

My voice is low in this bubble I've created between us, because the rest of the story needs to be told in the privacy of our own moment.

"When her dad came, Lillybeth screamed like she was being devoured by wild animals. She didn't move, her body was too broken for her to actually flee but her eyes and her voice were loud enough to tell her story without a single word." Kissing her patch of unmarred skin, I take in a deep breath before I continue.

"Dr. Manchin, along with the surgeons from pedes and general, were in that operating room for sixteen hours trying to undo everything that had been done to her. But the problem was that without a clear idea of what she'd been through, it was like playing hide and seek with blinders on. Her spleen had burst, her internal organs had shifted, her intestines were punctured and ripped. Every time they fixed one problem, another organ failed. But River?" Tears fell like rivulets down her cheeks, pooling in the palms of my hands. "She was a fighter, that kid. Sixteen hours and more procedures than any human should be able to withstand, Lillybeth survived that surgery. She survived her injuries. With six broken bones, she went through all the rehabilitation she needed to walk again." I rubbed the tip of my nose lightly against hers and delivered the final blow.

"A year later, she was placed back with her mother, who had left her dad. But when he found out she was back home, he busted in through their front door and killed them both, then himself. Dr. Manchin, the hardass of the hospital, collapsed in the nearest chair and broke down when we heard the news." River is now sobbing in my arms and I just hold her as tightly as I can without hurting her.

“We suspected her father had been the abuser but neither she nor her mother spoke. Do you know what her mother told us?” River’s head snaps up as she realizes where this story is going.

“She fell.” Her words are barely audible.

“She fell.” I agree.

# Chapter Six

## River

Last night was… well, intense. In so many ways. My entire body aches as I struggle to stretch out my limbs.

Wait…?

Why am I struggling?

Oh my fucking God, Nathaniel stayed over! His heavy—and bare—forearm is resting over my hip, and I can feel the whisper of his hand hanging oh-so-close to my pussy. Which is, thankfully, covered by my bed shorts.

Opening my eyes, I slowly look down before gently rolling onto my front to slip away from his hold. It's not that I don't enjoy being held, but after two attacks in what feels like minutes apart, I'm feeling a little uneasy. On the edge of the bed, I slip one leg out, placing my foot onto the floor quietly, followed by the other leg, leaving me practically kneeling on the floor, with my head and chest still on the sheet. In another situation, it'd be the perfect time to give a blow job as my face is practically level with Nathaniel's—very erect—morning wood.

"Where do you think you're going?"

A deep, sleepy drawl interrupts my escape and I glance up. He has one eye open, looking across at me with a half smile playing on his lips.

"Just going to the bathroom." With a shrug and a small grin of my own—because smiling any more than this right now hurts like fuck—I play it off and continue to basically crawl backward off the bed.

"I do like you on your knees." Lifting his head, he rests it on his arm to get a better view, both eyes open now. All sleep disheveled, rumpled among my sheets in just his jeans, I can't help but admire how fucking gorgeous he is.

"Well, that's inappropriate." Standing, I turn and look over my shoulder at him, my intention is to wink, but fuck no. That requires cheek muscles that are too bruised for fun things like flirting, making me pause for a moment.

"How's your face this morning?"

The crinkle in his brow and sudden loss of smile tell me I didn't hide my wince very well.

"I think I'm ready to enter the Miss World Pageant, don't you?" Sarcasm is my best form of defense in an uncomfortable situation. My head is all over the fucking place and I'm angry as hell, but not at Nathaniel. What happened isn't his fault. I just can't be completely vulnerable in front of him. Not yet.

Last night was an exception, I was in shock.

It doesn't count.

"River." His tone is hard, unyielding, and completely out of character for him. Although, I'm assuming a lot of things with this man. Maybe, underneath the laid-back, doctorly façade, he's a control god waiting for the right occasion to unleash his dominant tendencies. "You don't need to put on an act and pretend with me. It's okay—"

"No." I can't listen to him talk about last night or tell me it'll all be okay. Because it won't be. It happened and there's fuck all I can do about it now. What I can do is move forward and make damn sure I'm never put in a situation like that again.

"No?" His amusement is laced with concern as he sits all the way up, leaning back against the deep-blue velveteen headboard with his very defined abs on show and his hands in his lap—my guess is he's trying to hide his morning glory. A memory of last night in my shower makes me smile. I was in shock, but that doesn't mean I didn't appreciate his toned, naked chest that's on display for me again now.

"Exactly." With a raised brow and a small nod, I head toward the bathroom, leaving him looking all sexy and rumpled in my bed. In my bed that has never had a man—other than Kai when he's visited—sleeping in it.

Once in the bathroom, I check my reflection out in the mirror.

*Shit.*

Although, it looks better than I thought it would. There's a purple bruise on my cheek with a small graze, and a deeper bruise on my brow, three stitches covering the cut and keeping a small amount of skin from flapping off. Lifting my oversized T-shirt, I peel away the dressing on my rib to get a better look.

Who would've thought being stabbed—even just a little bit—would look like a teeny scratch? It's only about an inch long, just enough for the tip to have penetrated me. I'm sure, one day, I'll find that funny.

After carefully showering, doing my business, and brushing my teeth, I exit the bathroom wrapped in a fluffy blue towel. Nathaniel is in the kitchen as I walk through, opening and closing cupboards as if he's searching for something. Probably some kind of sustenance.

I have none.

"Looking for the coffee?" I pause by the breakfast bar and rest my elbows on the surface. It's all I can do to not admire the way the muscles in his back flex as he moves around my kitchen.

"You're going to tell me you have none, aren't you?" As he turns to look at me, I notice the hitch in his breath and the held back shock in his eyes as he takes me in. My damp hair falling over one side of my face—not the damaged side as I didn't want to get my stitches wet—and my completely bare shoulders and arms on full display.

"I am. I had planned to get a few supplies last night, but..."

Fuck my life, being strong is hard. I clear my throat, ready to continue, but Nathaniel raises a hand.

"No... we'll go out and get some. I need to get a shower and a change of clothes first though." Closing the cupboard he was just peering into, he pats the breakfast bar and heads toward the bathroom.

Before I can reply, he stops mere inches from me, so close that I can feel the heat coming from his skin. Nathaniel Reed is nothing short of an Adonis, but there is a war raging in the depths of his ocean-blue eyes. We don't speak in those endless seconds, and his gaze roams my face as though he's taking inventory of every line and bruise on my skin. Finally, a small shake of his head tells me he's made a decision, but the frown says so much more. Like regret and midnight fantasies aren't supposed to mix.

His index finger rises to my wet hair, where he pushes a lone strand up and away before leaning in and kissing my crown on an exhale. "You look beautiful, River."

The moment is over as quickly as it began, and he really does head toward the bathroom this time.

Partially in shock, and knowing he's going to be in my bathroom again—naked this time—sends a lustful shiver up my spine that I really need to ignore. The same way I'm ignoring his comment about me being beautiful. With a purple welt on my cheek, I can't find it in myself to accept the compliment.

"Oh, and River?" He's standing in the doorway of my bathroom, half in, half out, throwing me an almighty smile that has me concentrating on not allowing my knees to buckle.

"Yeah?" *Is he going to ask me to join him?*

"You should get dressed." With a wink, he disappears, removing that fine ass from my sight and closing the door behind him.

The dominant vibes he was giving off last night are back, and I'm here for it.

Having him in my apartment like this should make me feel more uneasy than it does, but this man didn't need to take care of me. He could've just left me to it, let me deal.

And he didn't.

He brought me home, cleaned my wounds, and didn't force me to talk about what happened. I could see he'd wanted me to, and we both know he didn't believe my story about falling over, but he didn't push it. He showered me and told me the most heartbreaking story I've ever heard, and just let that sit between us. After all this, he followed me to bed and simply laid beside me. We were side by side, staring at the ceiling without saying a word for I don't know how long, as I allowed my tears to silently creep down my cheeks before falling asleep.

I'll be forever thankful for his kindness. I would've lived in my bed until my next booking if he hadn't been here this morning. Having someone around to be strong in front of actually helps me push aside the part of me that wants to break.

Shit gets thrown at everyone, if we all broke, the world would stop turning.

Dressed in black skinny jeans and a dusky pink off-the-shoulder sweater, I style my hair so the longer strands fall over the cuts and bruises on my face. It's not a complete cover-up, but it's better than nothing. Luckily, my next appointment with a client isn't until Wednesday, so I have a few days to let this heal.

"Ready to go, Skittles?"

I fucking love that nickname.

"Yeah. Just getting my boots on and I'm ready." Turning to face him, a smile escapes my lips. He's wearing the same clothes as last night; a white shirt with rolled-up sleeves, the top few buttons undone and showing a spattering of hair on his super-toned chest, and the jeans he's been commando underneath all night that hug his thighs and ass just right.

The stoop is empty as we exit my building, and Nathaniel does as he always does, offering his elbow for me to take, like the perfect gentleman.

Sipping coffees in paper cups from a vendor we passed on the way, I enjoy the comfortable silence with Nathaniel as we head to his apartment so he can change. I get the impression something's playing on his mind, but I don't want to talk about my shit, so I won't make him talk about his.

Instead, I people-watch. The streets of New York City are perfect for it, and I find myself eyeing a group of women laughing and joking with each other outside an office block. They're each dressed in what I'd describe as 'alternative' clothes, with splashes of neon color breaking up the blacks, and thick-soled boots with silver spikes. It's almost like they all went shopping together and decided matching was best. They could almost pass for an alternative girl band.

Ooh, maybe they are?

"River?"

Nathaniel's deep voice brings me back from my observations, and by the look on his face, this isn't the first time he's tried to get my attention. Giving him a sheepish smile, I shrug.

"Sorry. I was in a world of my own."

His brow quirks and his blue eyes deepen, but it's quick. Had I blinked, I would have missed it.

"Do you live far from here?" We've only been out a couple of times, so I have no idea where he usually rests his head at night. I haven't even asked, which is pretty shitty of me.

"Just around the corner. It's ideal as it's only ten minutes away from the practice."

His apartment is no bigger than mine. If I'm honest with myself, I'd expected some fancy penthouse with huge glass windows. But then, I need to remember that 'Doctor rich' isn't the same as 'Tyler Walker rich'.

"Make yourself comfortable, I'll just be a few minutes." Nathaniel gestures toward the deep-brown sofa before disappearing into what I'm assuming is his bedroom.

It feels strange to be in his space, like I'm intruding somehow. There's a dead plant in the corner of the living area, clearly long-forgotten, and I see a photo on the wall above it. He's standing next to a petite woman with short, dark curls, his arm around her shoulders as she cuddles into him. They both wear matching smiles on their faces. If I had to guess, I'd say this was the wife he mentioned, Angelica.

Seeing that photo gives answers to that intruding feeling I have. Angelica's aura is all over this apartment, almost like she was the last person living here and all the furniture is hers. All of Nathaniel's worried glances and furrowed brows feel like they make sense to me now. I know his wife died of the big C, and obviously that's going to eat a man from the inside out, but it doesn't feel like he's actually let her go properly yet. Although, who could blame him if he never does? There's no rulebook for how to handle grief.

No one person has the right to judge how another reacts to their own traumas.

The bedroom door clicks, and out walks Nathaniel Reed in all his clean-shaven, clean-clothed glory.

"I feel like I need to play some runway music for you to strut along to with the way you're leaning against that door frame." Scrolling through Spotify, I hit play from fifty-seven seconds in on Right Said Fred's *I'm Too Sexy*, and turn my volume up as high as it will go.

As I bounce my head to the beat, I smile as best I can and encourage Nataniel to move for me with a wave of my hand. It's basically the law to *catwalk* to this part of the song. We are both in dire need of some cheering up—or forgetting about the real world—and this is already making my soul happy.

The way he throws his head back and laughs shows off his prominent Adam's apple, and the sound ricochets through me like a rocket hitting all my erogenous zones one by one. Quickly steeling himself, he raises a brow and pouts his lips, tucking one hand into a belt loop before he actually does it.

He struts like the best of them.

And damn, that's sexy. If I wasn't already sitting down, I'd be falling on my ass.

He stops a few seconds later, but his brief stint on our makeshift runway is enough to have us both in fits of much-needed laughter.

"You're something else, River Fox." Sitting on the sofa next to me, he leans forward, resting his elbows on his knees as he turns his head to look at me. My feet are tucked underneath my ass, and I'm comfy as fuck. This is a nice couch.

"I am that." A small smile plays on my lips, *I am many many things and I wish I could tell you about them.*

His body language indicates he has something to say, something he wants to get off his chest, but he stops himself. I'm still not going to push him though, I have learned that it's best to give people the time and space they need to open up.

"Walk?"

"You just did that, didn't you?" Laughing at his awkward one-worded question, I push against his shoulder.

"Yeah, yeah." He laughs. "Come on. It's a Sunday afternoon and Central Park is calling our names."

We both stand, my hand accidentally brushing against his thigh as we do. He stiffens as I inhale at the unexpected touch. Being in close proximity to Nathaniel Reed causes my breaths to become shallow and rapid, and I swear he says something. Something I can't hear because the beating of my heart is all I can concentrate on. The tension in this room is palpable, and we need to start moving before I allow something I really shouldn't.

October is a great time to be in New York. The tourist crowds have dispersed and the hot, humid weather is behind us, making our walk through Central Park a lot more enjoyable. It's like something out of a Hallmark movie; the smiles, the awkward glances, the idle conversation. We'll have to do this again in December so I can pretend to be that small town girl, falling in love with the big city doctor under the mistletoe and random snowball fights.

Fuck, I did it again. Zoning out while he's talking to me is becoming a habit. He doesn't repeat himself though. Instead, he smiles at me, with a little pity in his eyes that I wish would disappear.

Ignoring it, I look over into the water as we stand in the middle of Bow Bridge, and it goes a long way to warming my soul.

"There's just something about the air here that hits differently. You know?" He's quietly nodding next to me as we lean over the edge, allowing me to bask in this moment.

"More coffee?" Turning to him a few minutes later, seeing him as lost in thought as I was, I rest my hand on his bicep—I won't say it's an accident that my palm landed there.

"Sounds like a plan." That beautiful grin of his spreads across his face as he places his own hand over mine, and in that moment, we both pause. The mid-day sun is hitting him just right, emphasizing those crisp, cerulean of his eyes. In the light of day, they are brighter, more vibrant. Or maybe it's because his pupil is barely visible in the rays of the sun. Fuck, he really is too sexy for his shirt. Or mine, to be honest.

My breath catches in my throat, and I go to move my hand away, but he wraps his palm around my wrist and pulls me into him, looking down to meet my gaze head-on. And it's then I see something else in his eyes, something that brings flashes of being in the shower with him last night back to the forefront of my mind.

*Lust.*

I know that look very well.

It must be the fresh air, or the famously romantic bridge we're standing on, but I find myself leaning forward, hoping he will do the same. Our breaths mingle as we come together, painfully slowly, and the combination of leather and mint he exudes fills my senses.

Our lips crash together, much like they did last night, our tongues both fighting for dominance. Only, this is much more than what we experienced in the shower. This time, I can feel everything.

He wraps his arms around my waist, lifting me to sit on the wall of the bridge so we're a more even height, then he continues ravishing my mouth. His tongue wraps around mine in a way that makes me melt into him, wanting—no, *needing*—more of him. Soft fingers stroke up and down my back and neck before tangling into my hair, and every touch sends a jolt right to my clit.

Tyler was the last man to affect me in this way. Causing me to get wet without having to lube up.

Slowly, the feral, desperate kiss settles into a more seductive one, where nothing is said but everything implied. Without words, he tells me he's enjoying exploring my mouth. I could stay here for hours, blanketed in this feeling of safety, and dare I think it... happiness? With a pull of my lower lip between his teeth, he begins to move away and I'm convinced it's done.

It's not.

He gives me one soft kiss on the side of my mouth, before continuing those soft kisses across to my jawline, making his way to my neck and bare shoulder. Tilting my head back, I allow a quiet moan to escape my lips. This truly is heavenly. My breathing is heavy, my breasts practically heaving against his chest as he stands between my legs. His hair feels so silky in between my fingers as I clutch at the strands, I'm basically giving him a freaking head massage at this point.

Then my fucking phone rings. Of course it does.

Having intimate moments and fucking people might be my job—and of course I don't completely hate it—but as far as real-life men go, Nathaniel is the first in a long time.

I just wish I could allow more.

Pulling away from each other, I give him an apologetic smile as I answer the phone. I don't need to be on call for Tyler anymore, so I only have my personal one with me today. It's an unknown number, so I'm hesitant about answering, but I don't want Nathaniel to ask questions about why I'm ignoring calls.

"Hello?"

Oh, fuck right off. Again? Nothing.

"Look, whoever this is needs to fuck off."

Still, nothing.

Nathaniel is looking at me with eyes full of concern now.

Double fuck.

In the past, these calls have been something I've ignored because they came with the territory, then something I was afraid of. But now? I'm just fucking angry.

"River, what was that?"

I'm still sitting on the wall, with Nathaniel between my legs, his hands resting on my hips.

"Nothing to worry about."

Those eyebrows of his lower again, it's becoming a bit of a habit with him when he's concerned or unhappy with something I've said.

"I don't believe you." His voice is lower than usual, with a hint of darkness I actually quite like.

"You don't have to. Come on, let's go."

Whoever that was is a fucking mood killer.

"River, yo—"

"Do you want to come to Staten Island with me on the 31st?"

*Fuuuuuuck.*

Why did I ask him that? I wanted to change the subject, and damn, that I did. I mean, would it really be such a bad thing if he came? I can invite friends over for Samhain, right?

He looks at me, a little confusion marring his features.

"Sure, I'm not on call this weekend, but why Staten Island?"

"It's where my brother lives, we always celebrate Samhain together."

I should stop talking, but it's like Pringles; once you pop, you can't stop. A lead weight sits in my stomach the more I talk about it. Kai will be there.

Fuck it, he has Freya. And Nathaniel is my friend, and I'm not doing anything wrong.

"What's Saarwee?"

His pronunciation makes me laugh, he's trying to repeat what I said, and he clearly has no clue. Not that many people do to be fair.

"You might know of it if I say Samhain, spelled S-A-M-H-A-I-N, but it's pronounced saah-win or saah-ween."

"That, I've heard of, but I still don't know anything about it."

While I'm glad to have changed the conversation from the phone call, I can't help but feel like I have dug myself into a little hole with this invite. But, it's done. I'm embracing the chaos of my own mind.

"Well..."

# Chapter Seven

## River

Turns out, I didn't need to tell Nathaniel anything about Samhain. He's one of those guys who researches everything.

"Do you really talk to the dead?" A raised brow and mirth dancing in his eyes tell me everything I need to know.

He's skeptical.

"Did you read that on Samhain dot com?" I throw him a matching raised brow to let him know that his skepticism is shared but for a completely different reason.

It's a beautiful, crisp, fall day and we've just walked to the upper deck after leaving the car on the lower one. I love sitting up here, the view of Lower Manhattan—with its iconic skyline winking at me from the reflection of the sun's midday rays—is nothing short of breathtaking. It's a few minutes past one and although it's cold when the wind blows against my bare legs when directly under the sun's caress, it feels like the perfect temperature.

"Samhain for dummies dot com to be exact." Bumping his shoulder with mine, he gives me a devastating grin that makes my skin burn with all the dirty thoughts I'm starting to have about this man.

Is he gorgeous? Yes, a blind nun couldn't deny it. And I am neither blind nor a nun.

Yet, it's more than that. When he's with me, it feels like I am one hundred percent on his radar. Like I'm the most central person in his life.

It feels like I matter and I swear to fuck, that is as good as an orgasm.

"And that's what they said? That we talk to the dead?" He sits in a corner protected from the wind and as I move to take the seat next to him, he places both of his hands on my hips and pulls me down onto his lap, his arms wrapping protectively around me as I rest my head on his shoulder.

"Something like that. I think the word they used was 'communicating'." I scoff and shrug all at the same time because… leave it to the internet to reduce an age-old tradition to buzz words like "communicating with the dead". I suppose he'll just have to live it to understand it.

"This is nice." I don't mean to say it, I'm so used to keeping all emotion away from intimacy that I sometimes forget I'm allowed to have feelings with Candy Aisle Guy. I'm allowed to open up and be vulnerable.

I'm allowed to...

Except I have a job that would make this man—this honorable man—run for the hills, and that thought makes me feel queasy.

"I've never seen you wear this before." My nose is buried in the crook of his neck and his minty scent does things to me—wakens parts of my body that I long ago locked up—until I feel the very tip of his finger circling my skin where my Tiger's Eye crystal is resting just above my cleavage.

"My parents gave it to me. Everest has one similar, but his is a bracelet." I reach up and double tap the light brown and black crystal that hangs from a simple black cord. A habit I've had since I first placed it around my neck.

"Does it mean something?"

"Protection." I barely whisper the words and with the wind whipping around us, I'm surprised he heard it.

He hums out his understanding before delivering the blow that makes my stomach drop every time they're mentioned.

"You know, you never talk about them." I sigh, not wanting to get solemn. Tonight, I'll have time to meditate with Everest and feel close to them, but not now. Not like this.

"It hurts to do it. I'm guessing about as much as it hurts you to talk about Angelica." He's quiet for a beat but then he places a kiss at my temple.

"Touché." That simple acknowledgement that we share the same kind of pain does things to me all over again. Despite the heavy subject, his presence—the sheer confidence of him—as he cocoons me in his arms while trying to get to know the most intimate parts of me, makes my emotions run a little deep.

As deep as Kai ever has.

"Nathaniel?" His name slips like a prayer between my lips.

"Yes?"

"You're getting hard." My words are whispered into his jaw, making his arms band tighter around me.

"You do this to me, River. Every fucking time." I love that his voice is hoarse, like he's fighting to keep his control reined in.

"Why haven't you tried to fuck me?" It's not a needy question, I'm legit curious. I know men desire me, I know what they like and even when I threw myself at him, he denied me. Granted, the circumstances were not ideal.

It's when he pulls back just enough to place his large palm and long fingers around my jaw that I realize there's something darker in this man, something not so sweet. Something that makes my pussy clench with need.

"Look at me, River." It's impossible not to. "Make no mistake. There's nothing I want more than to bury my cock in your pussy and feel you come all over me for hours and hours. I promise you, it's going to happen as soon as you're ready for me." Pulling my mouth to his, he licks a path between my lips before giving me a taste of what he's got in store for me. "But not a minute sooner."

His words, his kiss, his impossibly hard dick at my hip make me groan, not to mention wet as fuck.

"You're a tease, Nathaniel Reed." His deep, throaty chuckle is life.

"Now, tell me about Samhain." And this time, he pronounces it correctly, making me smile even more.

By the time we pull up to Everest and Petal's home, I've given Nathaniel the general gist of what he's about to experience. I knew it would be a tough sell. Doctors and scientists are harder to convince about our traditions; not that we need to convince anyone. It is what it is. But, to be honest, I don't need a lecture on the possibilities of this or that.

Nathaniel turns off the engine and faces me fully. It's impossible to look away when he's looking at me like this, like the entire world revolves around the next words I'll say to him. Like his focus is only on me, on my needs, on my thoughts.

"I know it's a little late to ask this but..." He shifts his gaze over my shoulder to my brother's house before sliding back to me. "Are you sure you want me to be here? I get that it's something personal and family based."

Fuck, this man.

Reaching out, I wrap my fingers around his hand and squeeze.

"I want you here. It's just..." It's my turn to shift my gaze, but I decide in that second that he needs to know what he may walk into. "I've never brought a man to meet my family, so there may be suspicious looks from the guys and lots and lots of questions from my sister-in-law." My smile is instant at the thought of Petal asking him about his ascendency. Jesus, he's going to run away within the first thirty minutes.

"The guys? You mean your brother?" Fuck, I should have warned him about Kai, but I'm so used to keeping my two worlds separated that it's never a natural instinct to talk about him.

"And Kai. He's..." How the fuck do I describe him? "He's been my best friend since we were kids. His fiancée, Freya, too." Those last words feel like acid on my tongue.

Leaning in, he brushes his nose against my temple and murmurs quietly, "I'll have you know, brothers love me." I scoff because I'm sure they do. The normal brothers who don't smoke weed half the day and don't talk about the energy of the wind on his crops.

"Just remember..." Sinking my fingers in his hair, I pull him just enough to slide my lips against his in a soothing touch before I knock his ego down a notch. "Your medical degree won't impress anyone here."

His chuckle feels like sunshine on my skin.

"Well fuck, that was the only ace I had up my sleeve. I'm screwed now." Shaking his head, he pecks me on the cheek. "Come on, let's see if I pass the family test."

I don't wait for him to come around to my side of the door, by the time he runs around, I'm already out. Grabbing the handle before I have the time to close it, he pins me against his car and whispers in my ear. "Skittles, next time, I need you to let me open the door for you."

I grin. "Aw, you're such a gentleman." I run my hands up his chest and curl my fingers around the fabric, pulling him in until our mouths are mere inches away. "That's so fucking hot."

"Come on, little vixen." Taking my hand, his fingers wrapping around mine and squeezing, he pulls me up the driveway where Kai's truck is parked, the obelisk amethyst—to relieve stress and disperse his environment of negative energies—hanging from the rear-view mirror. I gave him that crystal months ago when he was working too hard and sleeping little.

Shaking the thoughts from my head, I remind myself that he's getting married and now I can move on with my life.

Looking up to Nathaniel, I smile. "Ready to be judged?"

He grins. "I love being judged and proving them wrong." I laugh at that because he has no idea what he's getting himself into.

"I hope you're not offended by weed." I barely hear his *oh shit* before the door is thrown open and a vibrant, big-smiled, Petal is rushing into my arms.

"My beautiful sister, it's been too long. Let me look at you." Most people, when they say this, quickly take you in to see that you're okay. Not Petal. When she wants to take a look at you, she's assessing your aura, your feelings, your mental health. It's uncanny but I quickly got used to it a long time ago.

"What happened?" My hand automatically flies to my brow and I hate that I didn't have the time for it to heal completely.

"It's nothing."

"That's not what your aura says, River. We'll talk about this later and I'll give you a spray with the Florida water. Ooh, and thank you so much for my birthday present! I've been trying to find the right Tibetan Singing Bowl, one that calls to me, you know? And as usual, you chose perfectly." She hugs me again before turning to Nathaniel and her eyes light up with pure happiness and curiosity.

"Petal, this is Nathaniel Reed, my..." I take a deep breath and say the words that make me a normal girl of twenty-six. "My date."

Petal squeals. Fucking squeals like I just told her I saved a puppy from being run over. Without hesitation, she places both of her tiny hands on Nathaniel's cheeks and looks at him. Really looks at him.

"Oh, you are bright inside." Her smile falters just a microsecond before she whispers, "I'm so sorry for your loss." Nathaniel visibly flinches, his smile wavering, his naturally smiling eyes clouding over, turning his ocean blues into a rolling storm.

I think he's in shock when he whispers back, "Thank you."

Yeah, Petal has that effect on people. You can't tell her to mind her own business because her intentions are always, always, pure.

Movement from my periphery forces my gaze to rise and the moment I do, I regret it.

Kai is standing on the landing—face impassive, hand raising a bottle of organic beer to his lips—watching like he has a million things he wants to say to me. I smile at him like my heart wasn't shattered all those weeks ago when he announced his engagement out of the fucking blue.

I even fucking wave at him like nothing is wrong. Like we're still besties. He's about to wave his own hand when Freya sidles up to him and wraps her arms around his waist. I think I see him flinch but I'm pretty sure that's my imagination.

"Come on, Ginny and Brad are waiting for us to harvest and I have a feeling we'll need to explain a whole lot of things to mister non-believer over here." Nathaniel chuckles at her words and mutters a quick, "I'm open minded, I promise."

We both scoff at that.

"We'll see." When I look up at him, all thoughts of Kai dissipate for the briefest, most soothing of seconds, as Nathaniel gives me a boyish grin that makes him look ten years younger. Fuck, this man is gorgeous.

Reaching Kai and Freya, I make quick introductions and hold my breath, feeling like my two worlds are colliding like a meteorite on Manhattan in some apocalyptic blockbuster movie.

It all feels like it's happening in slow motion.

Nathaniel holds out his hand for Kai to shake.

Kai hesitates. It's brief and only I can see it.

Their hands clasp and they squeeze, shaking once before releasing their holds. Nathaniel turns to Freya to say hello but Kai's gaze is locked on Nathaniel, eyes roaming his face, his hair, his body, before slicing his scrutiny over to me. I'm expecting anger and judgment but what I see is horror—my bruises are fading but the wounds are unmistakable—followed by hurt swimming in the dark honey of his irises.

That's rich. He's hurt? He's allowed to get engaged, but I'm the bitch if I bring a date to Samhain?

My discomfort turns to determination. Nope, not happening this way. I'm not here to make him jealous, I didn't bring Nathaniel to play some stupid game. I brought him because his company soothes me. Because being with him doesn't hurt. Quite the opposite, really.

Narrowing my eyes on Kai, I smile, and this time it's not the one filled with gratitude like the one I offered Nathaniel. This one says, "Fuck off with your own pity party."

"Hi Freya, you look great." She does, as always. Thick dark hair that falls just above her ample chest and curls at her cleavage like an arrow.

"Aw, thanks River. What happened to your face?" It sounds harsh but this is Freya, she doesn't always measure her words and I take it at face value.

"I fell." Nathaniel squeezes my hand and he has no idea how stabilizing that simple move is for me. How anchoring his reassurances are in this moment.

"Bullshit." Kai's arm shoots out, his fingers gently gripping my chin to turn right then left. "You don't get those kinds of bruises by falling, Riv." Then he turns my head so I'm staring only at him. "What happened?"

Nathaniel releases my hand and curls his arm around my waist, pulling me into him, his body angled in a way that Kai has to release me. "Don't worry, Kai. I'm taking care of her."

Kai's glare turns to Nathaniel and just as he's about to say something that will inevitably ruin this day, Everest comes barreling over with a roar of laughter.

"What the fuck you all doing at the door? We have shit to do." And just like that, the tension falls as everyone disperses to get ready to leave for the harvest. Petal brushes a hand on my arm as she passes, her way of telling me it's all going to be okay. I almost believe her.

"You all right, Skittles?" Bless this man.

"Yeah, I'm good." I scoff like it's no big deal. "Protective best friends and all that shit."

He doesn't believe me, but he's smart enough to know this isn't the place to have any kind of conversation that would unpack the history behind that interaction.

But I'm guessing that conversation will happen, and very soon.

# Chapter Eight

## River

It took us three hours to do what normally takes us less than two.

Brad and Ginny used to be hotshot lawyers in the Boston area but about four years ago, Brad suffered a heart attack that scared the living fuck out of Ginny, and with cause. Brad is thirty-eight but his heart was going on eighty with the hours he was putting in at the office. Ginny was just slightly less overworked. Having children had never been on their radar. Ginny didn't feel the gnawing need to be a mother and Brad once told us that the only need he had was to love Ginny and make her happy.

And let's be clear, these two are the poster kids for happy. Yes, Petal and Everest are sickeningly in love, but Brad and Ginny gave up their careers to make sure they could live happily together. They took their money and invested in land just outside of Staten Island. They rent out plots for communal farming and the rest they sell to local shops or farm-to-table delivery services. Last year, they started organizing trips for elementary school kids to spend the morning or afternoon learning how to plant, take care of, and harvest their own vegetables.

They don't make millions but they make enough to live comfortably, especially since Brad knows how to invest properly.

"Now I understand why you insisted I wear old jeans tonight." Nathaniel is grinning like a kid as he carries his loot of zucchini and squash while I share the burden of a box of pumpkins with Petal.

"There's something freeing about working the land, putting your fingers into the soil and birthing the fruit of its labor." Petal leans forward and looks directly at Nathaniel as she says her next words. "It's no coincidence that giving birth is called labor." I can practically feel my Candy Aisle Guy rolling his eyes as he corrects Petal.

"It's called labor because the whole process of giving birth is a lot of *work.*" I love that his tone isn't condescending, but the mirth in his eyes says he's calling bullshit on Petal's view of the world.

"Tomay-toe, tomah-to."

"Which we could have harvested tonight but there weren't any last minute tomatoes left." Everest is suddenly behind Petal and me, taking our big box and carrying it like it weighs nothing.

"That being said, I do believe that working the land is good for the soul." I grin at that, and because he makes Petal giggle, I decide he might just get laid tonight.

After thanking Brad and Ginny profusely for their hard work all year so we may have our harvest, we head back home. Each of us has a job to do and we easily fall into our routines without a second thought.

Petal and Freya get busy making dinner, their soul cakes and Barmbrack breads already cooling on the racks.

Everest and Kai are working on the final touches of the mulled wine and mead while I show Nathaniel how we like our home decorated. We set up the outside with our campfire ready to be lit as soon as we're finished eating.

"There are only six of us, you have nine plates here." This is the moment of truth. Either this man embraces the heart of Samhain or he runs for the ferry.

"Yes, six of us, my parents, and..." Fuck, I may have assumed too much or stepped on his toes with this, but he either takes me for who I am completely or we part ways now. "And Angelica."

The transformation doesn't happen right away. It's a gradual change from happy and carefree, curious and accepting, to completely closed off with a cinderblock wall separating us.

"What?" It's only a whisper, but the mixture of animosity and hurt is so loud I flinch.

"We set out a place at the table for our departed loved ones. I thought—" Nathaniel steps back—his hand shooting between us so I don't finish my phrase—nodding like he understands but at the same time can't wrap his head around what I was about to say.

"No." It's all he says, and I get it. It's too soon. When you haven't grown up with our traditions, it's difficult to embrace the idea that those we loved can cross the veil and brush up against us for just one special night. I know it sounds crazy but it's the only reason I survived my parents' deaths without completely losing my mind.

"Natha—" I watch him as he shakes his head, hands planted on his hips, begging me with his gaze to not continue this conversation. "Okay, I'll take the plate away." He nods once, then turns and walks out the door.

"You okay?" I turn when I hear Kai's voice behind me, nodding as I stare at the spot where Nathaniel was standing just moments ago.

"Yeah. I'm good." He comes to stand shoulder to shoulder with me and his proximity makes me ache with his betrayal, but also with his concern. And that's just the thing, isn't it? He'll always be concerned about me, he'll always have this little piece of me and I a piece of him, no matter what happens in our lives. Marriage, children, drama, it doesn't matter.

We have a titanium bond that started under the stars and will forever be a direct link to our hearts. Except, when Freya comes to stand beside him—her arms an unbreakable clamp around his waist—that bond mollifies, just a little, giving me room to walk away so I can apologize to Nathaniel.

"What are we looking at?" At the sound of her voice, I'm glad I'm already halfway to the back door.

I hear Kai call out my name just as Freya tells him to come help her with a "thing".

Ignoring them both, I step outside and look from left to right until I see the dark figure at the corner of the property. As I slowly make my way to Nathaniel, I rehearse my speech in my mind, focusing on the different ways I can say I'm sorry for assuming, for imposing, for meddling. Just as I reach him, he speaks without even turning around.

"When I first met Angelica, it was a family function. She had just graduated high school and I had finished up my sophomore year at John Hopkins." He pauses, and I'm not sure what I'm supposed to do. Do I offer him comfort? Do I stand here, behind him? I don't want him to stop talking so I sit on the grass, cross-legged, and listen.

"My God, she was radiant. I remember her smile had made me freeze mid-sentence with my father when I saw her walk inside the fundraiser ballroom. She just had this brightness about her, like a white light surrounded her."

"Her aura." My words are whispered. It's rare to see white auras, and this coming from someone like Nathaniel who doesn't believe, it makes me sad that he didn't know.

"I didn't hesitate, didn't even ask around about her or try to figure out if she was seeing someone or how old she was. I went straight to her and introduced myself. Four years later, just a week after she graduated from New York University, we were married. Everything about us was easy, light. We never argued, we never got carried away. We just loved each other."

I nod, even though he can't see me. When he turns around to face me—his hands in his pockets and head hanging low—he closes the short distance between us and sits in front of me.

"River, I'm not a big believer in all of this but the mere possibility of her seeing me—happy and smiling and fucking carefree—with another woman, makes my already crushing guilt feel a hundred times more consuming."

Tentatively, I reach out and place his hand between both of mine. "I'm sorry." Squeezing my hold on him, I try to transfer all of my understanding and affection onto him. It's then that something occurs to me.

"Hold on…" Straightening my shoulders and cocking my head to the side, I allow my gaze to travel around Nathaniel's face. His guileless eyes, a brow rising in question when I pause. "Ballroom? Gala? John Hopkins? That's a lot of rich talk for someone who lives in Midtown in a shoebox apartment with a dead plant." And then that devastating smile that makes my pussy hungry splays across his face.

"I like my apartment." It's all he says before he pulls me to him so I'm straddling his waist, his hands on my hips.

"I'm sure you do, Nathaniel Reed." I gasp then slap his chest with mock anger and shock.

"Ow! Why are you getting so violent, Skittles?"

"If you tell me you're a Reed, as in Reed Industries, I will cut you." In a flash, I'm on my back, his entire body on top of mine, my wrists in one of his hands as his other caresses my cheek.

"I won't tell you I'm a Reed from Reed Industries." Fuck, his voice is like a drop of honey on my tongue, but when his thickening cock pushes against my needy pussy, I almost lose every ounce of control, ready to have him fuck me right here on my brother's lawn.

"Dinner's ready!" Saved by the angry tone of Kai's announcement.

"Coming!" I yell out, my eyes fixed on Nathaniel as he thrusts his hips one more time in warning. Or promise for later.

"Not yet, but you will." Definitely a promise.

"Better fucking not be." Fucking Kai and his Jeckel and Hyde personality.

Dinner goes off without a hitch, the two plates for our parents at the heads of the table while the six of us sit on either side. Freya talks a lot about her plans for the wedding and every time I look at Kai, he seems to be in pain. Like talking about these plans are making him physically ill.

Well, tough shit, fucker.

After dessert, Everest leans back on his chair and grabs Petal at the waist, placing her on his lap where she curls up like a sloth. They nuzzle and he whispers in her ear before she nods, giggling.

"If you're going to fuck, please, for the love of the goddesses, don't do it out in the open for your neighbors to see again." Kai is shaking his head as he pops a white raisin into his mouth, left over from the Barmbrack.

I gasp, throwing the first dried fruit I see on my plate. "Shut the fuck up! Oh my God, please tell me it wasn't the little kid." Petal's dark red cheeks tell me everything I need to know.

Nathaniel whistles and I clamp a hand to my mouth. "That kid's gonna need a lot of fucking therapy after that."

"I think his mother is the one who's gonna need some serious couples' therapy because she was not looking away." Everyone around the table is laughing, Petal snorts as she wipes the tears from under her eyes.

Ah, good times.

"You ready, Riv?"

And so it begins. "Yeah, Ev, let's do this." With a long kiss, Everest puts Petal back in her chair like she's his favorite sack of potatoes.

"Love you, Pet." I swear, their love will give them cavities.

Reaching back, Everest grabs his baggie full of perfect green and orange heads with his special Samhain pipe, and we head outside to the small shrine we set up soon after they moved into the house. It's nothing religious, just a wooden table we prepped so it can stay outside under the willow tree. That tree is one of the reasons they chose this house. On top of the table is a ceramic statue of an elephant. It took us forever to finally decide on what to put here, but we both agreed that elephants were gentle and family oriented which was pretty perfect for our parents. I may not have been a fan of our lifestyle, but their love for us was real.

So fucking real.

"Pack it up, big sister."

For the second time tonight, I find myself sitting cross-legged on the grass, except this time I'm picking at the heads of the buds to pack the pipe. I use the back of my lighter to push down the fresh cannabis and breathe in its delicious, fresh scent.

"This smells so good. Where did you get it?" I look up at Everest and gasp when he grins like a Cheshire cat.

"You are not!"

"Sure am, little River."

"Nice!" We both nod as I light the green goodness. "Be careful, though, okay?" Ev shrugs as he lays out on the grass looking up at me, questions swimming in green eyes the same shade as mine.

"Just say it." I inhale, hold my breath, then slowly exhale.

"Wanna talk about it?" My little brother is seldom serious. However, right now, he's deadly.

Speaking while holding your breath is never easy, unless you're a stoner. "About what?"

"Don't do that. I may not always seem observant but I promise you, I see you." I raise my brow on an exhale, sure the confusion is written all over my face.

"Um, I see you, too?"

"Jesus, are you high already?" I turn my entire body to face him, handing him the pipe.

"No, smartass. We don't hang out enough for me to decipher your philosophic bullshit."

"Okay," Ev inhales before speaking again. "I'll be blunt. If that dude did that?" He points to my battered face, "I'll fucking kill him."

It takes my brain a moment to register his words. Everest is many things but violent, he is not.

"Oh my goddess! No. Jeez, do you see me inviting a guy who's just beat me up to Samhain? I'm offended." Passing me the pipe once again, he props up on his elbow and shakes his head.

"Nah, but I got a vibe from him and, you know, sometimes, people believe their own lies."

I snort. But of course, it's at the wrong time and my coughing fit begins, making my eyes water and my head throb. "I love you, little brother. I really fucking do. I promise, it's not him. He actually healed me all up." We both lie down, staring at the twinkling stars shining through the falling leaves and losing ourselves to the buzz.

"So, he's a doctor, huh? Like a real one?" It's my turn to shrug.

"I like him."

"I mean, I get it. For sure, you know? But he's never going to understand our way of life."

I take in a deep breath of cool night air.

"I'm not marrying him tomorrow, goofball."

"I dunno, Riv. He looks like he's hooked, man. I mean, Samhain isn't for the faint of heart." I laugh because, what the fuck does that mean?

"We're not sacrificing young lamb, Everest. Damn, what the fuck kind of bud is this?" Now, we're both laughing.

"I'd never sacrifice a lamb. Maybe a hyena, those fuckers are weird looking and mean. I saw this documentary once and they—"

"Fucking hell, Ev, no. I'm not sitting here talking hyena documentaries with you. Come on, let's go say hi to them."

Crawling on hands and knees—walking is too difficult—we sit in front of the statue and close our eyes. There's no summoning or witchy shit going on. We're just two kids, high on good weed and wanting to feel close to their dead parents.

It's what we do.

I'm feeling great, light, floaty, when the first grunt happens, accompanied by a faraway shriek. I'm confused because it's not part of our tradition, the whole grunting, screaming thing.

Then a thought occurs to me. What if Freya and Kai are fucking around the camp fire? Like literally fucking. While Nathaniel is watching. What else is he supposed to do?

What if he likes it?

Another grunt, except this doesn't sound like pleasure... unless Freya is into some dark shit.

"You motherfucker!" Yeah, definitely not fucking.

"What the fuck?" I open one eye to see Everest slowly rising to his feet.

"Your boy is about to beat the shit out of Kai."

Moving as fast as my heavy legs will take me, I yell at Nathaniel just before Petal reaches the two men squaring off.

"You will stop this, right now. I will not have this negative energy on my land, in my home. You will respect Samhain or else leave. Do you understand?" She immediately starts spraying them both with her Florida water as I come to a halt, nearly falling on my face when my toe hits a small rock by one of the human-sized pillows. Nathaniel and Kai both reach for me, I'm guessing to make sure I don't hit the ground, but I must not be as high as I'd hoped because I'm able to steady myself on my own.

"What's going on?" My gaze travels from Nathaniel's icy stare-down with Kai, who looks ready to murder someone, and then Freya, who's shooting daggers at me. What the fuck did I do?

"Come on, brother, you need to cool off." Everest takes Kai by the back of the shirt and pulls him just as he leans down and kisses Petal square on the mouth. "You okay, Pet?"

"Yes, I'll be just fine." Then she turns to Freya with a more subdued tone and tells her—nicely—to move the fuck on.

"I'm sorry you had to see that, Nathaniel. Her aura is such a bright red most times but tonight, with the alcohol, she was bordering on brown. Never a good sign." Nathaniel blinks—still staring at Kai as he's pulled away from the scene—and I'm pretty sure he has no idea what Petal is talking about. Stepping in front of him, I reach up on my tippy toes and place both of my hands on his face, forcing him to look down at me.

"Hey! Petal and I will clean up, you go up to the room, okay? Second door on the right. Do you mind grabbing our bags?" He nods, practically robotic, but with enough wherewithal to grab me by the back of the head and kiss me with a passion that literally makes my knees give out.

Still, he's got me. I hear Petal sigh dramatically beside me, then he's gone.

"What the hell happened?" I whisper-yell at Petal, trying to wrap my head around what just went down.

"It seemed so insignificant at first. Nathaniel was watching you, I think he was really interested in the trad—"

"Focus, Pet!"

"Okay, so, Kai said something about us being really protective of you." I frown, not understanding why this would set Nathaniel off.

"But then Freya—she was drunk by the way, which is why I'm not a fan of day drinking—jumped in and told Kai that he was the one protective of you and that he was engaged to her and he should be paying attention to her not you." Still, this wouldn't make Nathaniel so upset. What the fuck?

"So Kai tells her to settle down and he turns to Nathaniel telling him that if he finds out that he's the one who hurt you, he'd fucking kill him." I gasp right before my mind wanders to the moment Everest said the same thing.

"Wow, they really are like brothers."

"And that's when Freya opens her big drunk mouth and screams that of course he would, and was he still fucking you." The groan escapes from between my lips and kills my buzz.

Fuck. My. Life.

"Yeah. It was all so negative. Just a lot of walls building, good energy being sucked away."

"I'm so sorry, Petal. I shouldn't have brought him. He doesn't deserve this." Or maybe I should have kept him close the whole time, but fucking hell, I'm not his babysitter.

"No, River," Petal places a soothing hand on my arm and does what Petal does best. Squeezing lightly, she infuses me with her warmth and love. "You deserve to be happy and I promise you, Nathaniel has this gray aura that is in need of your blue. You're perfect together." I smile, grin actually, because I really needed to hear this. Also, I'm still high.

"You're right."

"Yeah, and..." she whispers her next words because sending negativity into the world isn't her jam. "Fuck Kai. He made his own bed, now he needs to sleep next to her in it."

Petal and I clean up and honestly, I have no idea where Everest took Kai and Freya, but I don't care either. We take in the covers and pillows, the chill of the air making my skin pebble with goosebumps.

There are a couple of bottles of mead lying around. Grabbing them with my free hand, I make it to the kitchen after dropping the pillows onto the couch. The recycling bin is almost full but I'm too tired to transfer it all outside. The last of the dishes are now in the washer, the pots and pans washed and drying on the side.

"You didn't waste any time, did you?" I spin around, frowning, my hand clutching the edge of the counter. I didn't hear him come in and I swear the feelings of the other night, the surprise and shock, come rushing back to me.

"Excuse me?" Kai is standing at the entrance of the kitchen, hands in his pocket, eyes on me so intense that I'm not sure if it's hurt I see or anger so fiery it burns me from afar.

"Tyler Walker. Was he just your flavor of the month? Or maybe you like to switch it up every two weeks?" I could kill him right now.

"You're one to talk. How's the wedding planning going?" Oh God, I didn't mean to say that.

"You have no idea what you're talking about." Kai stands straighter, like he's getting ready for a fight. Well, asshole, let's go.

"Are you not getting married? To Freya?" He has the decency to look down, his shoulders losing a little of the cocky attitude.

"That's what I thought."

Grabbing two glasses of water, I head for the door, hoping he'll move out of the way so I can pass, but knowing him well enough to know that he won't.

*Bingo.*

His fingers wrap around my bicep, not hard enough to hurt but enough to stop me in my tracks.

"I called you the other night." His gaze is searching my face, my eyes, my mouth.

"I know."

"Why didn't you answer my calls?" The crease between his eyes deepens with every word.

"I was busy."

"Did he do this to you?" His question takes me aback. Not because of the words, but his tone. His voice breaks on the last one, like putting the idea out into the universe actually shatters him. "I promise you, I'll kill him if he did."

"Kai, no. He was there for me. He healed me." I stare into his honey orbs and get lost for a moment, remembering us. That titanium grows stronger and I lose a little of my fight, too.

"Don't do this, River. Just, wait for me." His words are whispered, the last syllable cracking with his pain. I don't understand it.

"What? No, Kai. I'm not going to wait for you. Did you wait for me?" Now I'm pissed all over again. "Did you wonder what it would feel like to hear her announce your fucking engagement? Did you?" I try to get out of his hold, but it's no use.

"Well, it's not like you weren't already a little busy fucking the rich one." I don't think. I just act.

One of the glasses I'm holding is full one second and then all its contents are on Kai's face.

"Fuck you, Kai. Fuck you for doing it all wrong and trying to blame me for it. Fuck you and your high horse. Fuck you and your belief that I should just stay home and wait for you to make up your mind. Would I even be allowed to masturbate or would I need your permission for that too?"

"River—"

"No. Go to your fiancé and leave me the fuck alone."

"River."

I don't bother answering as I hurry up the stairs and into my bedroom—perks of having my own room at my brother's house.

# Chapter Nine
## River

Opening my bedroom door, I'm so fucking angry, I'm panting, my breaths coming short and heavy. Fuck Kai and all his bullshit. I love the man, but fuck me, he's the most confusing asshole on the planet.

What was it Petal said? *"He's made his own bed..."* So I'm going to make mine.

Nathaniel is sitting on the armchair in the corner of the room, and as I storm in, he looks up, forehead creasing in concern as his eyes lock with mine.

"River, wha—"

"No."

The concern on his face quickly turns to one of amusement as he raises a singular sexy motherfucking eyebrow at me.

"No?" The corner of his eye creases as he gifts me a half-smile.

"Yes. No." I punctuate my "no" by quickly unclipping my overalls, flinging the straps over my shoulders, and letting them fall to my ankles, leaving me in just my tight white T-shirt and panties. Crossing my arms over myself, I grab the hem of my shirt and pull it over my head. My bra is thin lace, so it's pretty see-through and Nathaniel likely has a good view of my nipples—they're standing to attention so hard, they'd be difficult to miss.

But he's not looking at my nipples, or anywhere below my face. His eyes are boring into mine with nothing but volcanic heat behind them. Can't say I hate it. It actually sends a thrill right through me, and I have to suppress a shiver trailing down my spine.

Slowly making my way over to him, I trail my hands up and down my front, between my breasts and around my nipples, before bringing a finger to my mouth and gently sucking on it. His pupils are dilated as he sits there, his hands splayed out on each arm rest, his legs slightly apart—enough room for me to nudge my own leg between them.

Bending down in front of him, my chest practically in his face, I take hold of his hand, and slide it up from my thigh, over my stomach, between my breasts and landing on my throat. His hold there, under my own hand, feels like he knows what he's doing. There's a correct way to hold someone by the throat, and the tension in his hand is that of a pro. The feeling makes my nipples pebble impossibly harder, and I'm sure my panties are soaked right now. Pulling at his hand, I single out his index finger and slide it into my mouth as I straddle him, one leg on either side of his thick thighs.

His rock-hard cock is straining against his pants, and his fingers still on the arm of the chair are clenched so tightly his knuckles are white. Swirling my tongue around the tip of his finger, I move my hips a little, just enough to feel him against me as I slowly bite down, testing his limits. Limits which, if the look in his eyes is anything to go by, he doesn't appear to have.

Pulling his finger out of my mouth with a *pop*, I push it downward, trailing my own spit between my breasts to the top of my panties. Before I can move it lower, Nathaniel pulls his hand away and grips my hips, resting his head against my chest, our ragged breathing the only sound in the room.

I'm still high as fuck, and I'm not sure if I'm doing the right thing here with Nathaniel, but I'm not a quitter and I've started something now that I refuse to stop. It feels too damn good.

A low growl coming from his chest surprises me—but fuck, it's hot—before he dips his head lower and licks a slow path from my belly button to my nipple.

It's fucking tortuous in the best possible way. My panties are soaked from the attention on my nipple alone, and I let out a groan of appreciation as he continues his onslaught. Nipping and flicking, and showing me just what he can do with that delicious tongue of his. The tension inside me is building, his grip unrelenting, and just as I think I'm about to come, he stops.

Fucking stops.

A groan of sexual frustration leaves my mouth as he places light kisses across my chest and up to my neck, where he stops again, his warm breath against my ear.

"What's your safe word?"

Wow. I wasn't expecting this from him, but the thrill swirling around my clit fucking loves it.

"I don't have one." My voice is breathier than I expected, and he shudders underneath me. Staying perfectly still as he speaks again.

"You're gonna need one, Skittles. Choose. Now. Or I'll do it for you."

Okay, so I do have a regular safe word, one that is written into contracts and discussed with my clients, and I know changing it now would be a bad idea as I'd likely forget it. Not that I think I'd ever have to use it with Nathaniel, but it just feels different discussing a safe word with, well, not a client. Fuck it.

"Simba."

As he pulls away from my neck, he doesn't look horrified by my choice of word like I thought he would. He just nods—one simple nod of the head—before he stands, lifting me with him, wrapping my legs around his waist as he takes hold of my ass. Walking us over to the bed, which is only a few short steps, he buries his face in my neck again and inhales deeply before throwing me onto the sheets. My back hits the mattress and I bounce once, watching as he starts to pace the room.

After scooting up to the pillows, I sit up a little so I can see him better. This is like a goddam show, I have no idea what he's about to do next, I just know it's going to be fucking good. The anticipation for what is about to happen is thrumming through my entire body.

"Bra, off." It's almost like he can't form a full sentence right now, his voice is so deep and throaty and fucking intense.

Doing as he asks, I arch my back—it's really unnecessary but I do it anyway—thrusting my breasts forward as I reach around to undo my bra. Slowly, I slide each strap down my arms, one by one, until I'm bare to him. Well, apart from my panties, but they're so wet at this point I think they're see-through.

As I'm doing this, he's still pacing the room. No, stalking. Like a predator stalking his prey as he grabs the back of his shirt at the neck and pulls it over his head, discarding it to the side. His chest is a fucking work of art, with just the right amount of hair across his well-defined torso. It's all hard ridges and dips that I really want to lick. But I get the impression Nathaniel likes to be in charge, and tonight, I'll give him that.

For once, I don't want to be in control. For once, I want to give the reins of responsibility to someone else.

"Take off your panties. Slowly."

"These?" Playing with the top of my panties, I look at him through my lashes, letting one hand slide further down toward my clit.

"I said, panties, off. I did not give you permission to touch yourself. Do you understand?"

Holy shit, do I ever! All the *'Yes, Sirs.'*

I nod with a raised brow, fucking loving this side of him. And his returning smirk is a thing straight out of my wet-dreams.

Sliding my panties down my legs, I bend my knees and bring them up to my chest, giving him the perfect view of my naked ass, both of my holes visible to him as I pull my panties all the way past my ankles. The sharp intake of his breath as I slowly lower my legs and leave my knees slightly apart for him, makes my entire body burn.

His stalking around the room continues, like a wild lion, and he unbuckles his belt painfully slowly, before popping the button of his jeans, followed by the zipper... and finally, he lets them fall to his feet.

Well, it looks like tonight is full of surprises.

Nathaniel Reed is commando.

His thick cock is so hard it's touching his belly button, and I can see beads of pre-cum dripping from his slit. The sight sends another thrill through me and I lick my lips in anticipation. It's something I know would have driven him wild had he seen it, but his eyes are darting from side to side, all around the room. Searching for what, I have no idea. Determination is written all over his face as he stops at the foot of the bed and looks up, his gaze catching mine just as he takes hold of his cock.

Watching a man stroke himself is one of the sexiest things I've seen, and I've seen a lot. The way his pupils dilate, his hitches, and the pure lust written in every move he makes has my clit pulsing in anticipation with what's to come, and I trail my hand across my stomach as I watch.

He sinks his teeth into his lower lip when he sees what I'm doing, his eyes narrowing in on where my hand is paused, hovering just above my pussy. That sexy-as-sin growl comes from deep within his throat as he looks around again. His movements stop, his face brightening just before he bends to pick something up from the floor, giving me a perfect view of his peachy ass.

As he rises to his full height, one hand still wrapped around his thick cock, he lifts his other arm, a maniacal smile on his beautiful face, and I realize what he's holding.

His belt.

Walking with measured movements around the side of the bed, slowly tugging at himself as he does, he gives me time to say no, or use my safe word. It's obvious what he wants to do with this belt right now, and I'm all for it. So much so, I even raise my arms above my head, ready for him.

He doesn't seem surprised by my action, like he knows he's found his sexual equal, and my own maniacal smile grows.

*Yeah, I'm all for this shit!*

"Good girl." He tilts his head in appreciation as he leans over to bind my wrists with his belt—like a fucking pro—and his cock is so close to my face I can almost taste it.

Lifting up as best I can, I open my mouth and lick the very tip, only to be pulled back down by where I am now bound.

"Did I give you permission to move, little vixen?"

He rises to his full height again, returning his hand to his cock as he does, drinking me in from head to toe with those blue-lagoon eyes of his. This is the most intense foreplay I've had in years, and I'm so needy right now I could come from just one more touch, I know it.

I shake my head, meeting his lust-filled gaze with my own.

"Words."

Every time he makes a demand, it's like he's lighting another match inside my body. All of them burning through me, just waiting for him to blow them out with his touch.

"No." My lips upturn into a small smile as I answer his question. This is so much fucking fun!

Literally. Fucking, fun.

A tingling sensation begins to run up my leg, and I realize he's now touching me. But it's so feather-light, he's barely connecting with my skin. He trails his fingers agonizingly slowly from my toes, up the inside of my leg, skipping the part where I really need his touch, and working his way up to my breasts. It takes a lot of fucking willpower to not explode everywhere and I arch my back to try and get him to brush against my nipples. I'm so worked up it'd be easy to just let go.

But I want more. I need more.

His eyes are following the trail of his fingers, and just as they reach a pert pink bud, he pinches it. I inhale sharply, letting out a low moan with my next breath, and the pleasure-pain sensation forces me to writhe, rubbing my thighs together for some friction.

"I love the way you moan. It might just become my new favorite sound."

Still slowly palming himself, he turns and walks toward the dresser. Holy shit, that ass. He's got to work out, there's no way his ass is that deliciously plump on its own.

"What are you doing?"

"You'll see." Slowly looking back over his shoulder, his eyes collide with mine once more. "This candle, what kind is it?" He holds up the burning red candle from my dresser, and now I'm really confused.

He wants to discuss candles?

"It's soy, Petal makes them."

The wolfish grin that graces his face when I give him the answer he so clearly wants to hear is like something from all my dirtiest fantasies. It's pure sex.

"Excellent."

Making his way back over, he places the candle on the bedside table before grabbing my ankles and spreading me out for him. Then he picks it back up and climbs on the bed, settling between my legs on his knees. I love that he's giving me time to say no to this, and though it feels like he's taking forever to get to the good stuff, this build up is fucking intense.

He brushes his lips against mine once he's got the candle, and I can feel his velvety cock stroke against my thigh as he leans back onto his knees in between my legs.

Wax play isn't something everyone is into, and Nathaniel being into it is just another thing I didn't know about this man. I'm excited to find out more. It seems he's a kinky fuck, and I certainly don't hate it.

"You're fucking beautiful. Lying there, spread open, that perfect little pussy on display and dripping for me." As he speaks, he's running one palm up and down my thigh, his fingers coming into contact with my clit for only brief moments.

Lifting my ass, I silently beg for more, closing my eyes and getting lost in the sensations. A sharp tap on my ass makes me open them again, and I'm sure my pupils are as blown as his.

"Eyes open, my little vixen."

With one last stroke over my clit, he brings his wet finger to his mouth and sucks.

"Fucking delicious."

I'm going to burst like a freaking volcano soon.

Bringing his wrist up, he slowly drips the pool of wax from the candle onto his skin, before nodding once, satisfied with the temperature.

"Hard limits?" He holds the candle over my thigh, and God damn this man. Usually this is something I'd have discussed with a client beforehand so there's no interruption during their time with me. But Jesus Christ, getting consent while we're already hot and heavy is fucking sexy.

"No wax on my pussy or ass."

After nodding once to let me know he understands, he begins to drip hot wax onto the top of my thigh. Just a few drops before he moves up to my stomach and chest, avoiding my nipples. The wax is painful as it hits my skin, but it's also relaxing and sensual and the feeling is like no other.

"Eyes on me, Vixen." He blows the candle out before continuing to slowly drip the pool of hot wax all over my chest and stomach.

The soft sheets beneath me feel like the Ying to the Yang of the wax on my front. His hand follows where the wax drips, circling each spot and enhancing the pleasure coursing through my body. When he's finished with the candle, he leans over me again, placing it gently on the bedside table.

This time, as he brushes his lips against mine, I raise my head, slipping my tongue between his plump lips and encouraging him to open up for me. I bring my bound arms down and over his head, wrapping my legs around his waist and feeling his delicious cock against my wet and needy pussy.

With a sharp bite on my lower lip, he slides his hands from my shoulders to my wrists behind his head, and gently lifts them, clasping my hands above my head once more.

"Patience." That raised brow and wolfish grin make my insides twist and burn hotter still.

It's then I realize he hasn't asked about protection, and though he's a doctor and likely takes care of himself, I'm not going bareback without having the conversation.

"Check the drawer in my bedside table." My voice is still breathy as fuck, but he'll find a little more in there than just condoms. I'm hoping he wants to keep playing.

Lifting one of my legs from around his waist, he licks from my ankle to my clit, before taking the other one to do the same. When he reaches my inner thigh, he pauses, taking note of the square patch of skin that doesn't match the rest. His features darken and his brow furrows, but only ever so briefly before he places a gentle kiss there.

Leaning over me again, his cock gliding against my stomach this time, he opens the drawer and takes a look inside. His eyes widen and his brows rise in a temporary shock, before a slow grin creeps onto his face and the crinkles at his eyes spell mischief. He pulls out three things; a condom, strawberry lube, and my favorite butt-plug. One Kai has admittedly had fun using on me in the past, hence it being in my drawer at my brother's house—and of course, it's always thoroughly cleaned after each use.

He holds it up for me as he drops back to his knees in between my legs.

"Interesting. Put your ankles on my shoulders."

His bestial grin and the dark look in his eyes say he's far from done playing with me. All this, and I still haven't come yet, I'm freaking dying here. Still, I do as he asks, placing my ankles on his shoulders and dropping my knees to the sides.

I'm wide open for him, and I can feel myself dripping through my folds.

"You're a dirty girl, aren't you? You like to be played with, little vixen?"

Eyes widening at my nod, he taps my ass, telling me he wants my words.

"Yes." My voice is breathy, barely audible, but it's enough.

"I'm going to fuck your delectable pussy with this in your ass. Show me that hole."

I lift my ass so it's level with his face, using him as leverage, and his eyes narrow in on me.

"Good girl."

I've never been called a good girl so often in my life, and I think I like it.

I kind of want to be his good girl.

This build up is fucking intense. My breaths heavy, my chest literally heaving, and my skin prickling with heat, I just need something inside me already. I don't care what or where it is.

He squeezes some lube on my puckered hole before rubbing it around with his thumb, and I groan so loud I'm sure the others in the house will hear us. I've been trying to stay relatively quiet until this point, but fuck it.

The intrusion against my hole is one of pure pleasure as he stretches me with his fingers. Using his other hand, he fingers my pussy, dipping in and out, spreading around my arousal and punching at my clit. It's enough to make me come undone, and I do.

Clenching my eyes closed, I fucking explode. It's intense, it's everything I've been wanting since we got naked, and I try to squeeze my thighs together as it's almost too much. Pins and needles spread through my body and he pinches my clit again, bringing my attention back to him.

"Eyes. On. Me. Understand?"

"Fuck, yes."

Removing his fingers from my ass, he picks up the bottle of lube again. The cold substance feels like it sizzles against my burning hot skin, and the shudder I can see rolling through his body makes me want to touch him, to feel him, to run my hands all over his soft skin and hard ridges. But this time, it's his show. I'll continue to be his good girl with my arms bound above my head.

The metal butt-plug is at my entrance next. First, he slides it all over my wet pussy, using my cum as a natural lube. Then, he places it against my ass and slowly pushes it inside, at the same time as peeling a few joined drips of wax from my thigh. The stretch of my ass from the butt plug counteracts the tingling and satisfying pleasure from the wax being peeled away.

Once the plug is fully seated, Nathaniel growls low, the sound coming from deep within his chest.

"So fucking sexy with that little red gem next to your perfectly wet pussy."

Grabbing my ass cheeks, he kneads them roughly, lowering me back to the bed and following me down as he goes. His head is still level with my pussy, and he uses that to his advantage, running his tongue all over me. He sucks and bites at my clit, pushes his tongue inside me, then brings a finger or two to the party down there.

I fucking explode again, all over his face. Bringing one hand up to squeeze my breast and pinch my nipple, he groans as he laps me up. My body twitches in glorious pleasure with every stroke of his tongue, and just as another orgasm builds to an almost excruciating high, he stops. Lifting his head, he runs his tongue over his lips.

"Mmm, fucking delicious."

His eyes are on mine as he rips open the foil and rolls the condom down his thick cock before he grabs my hips and pushes the head of his cock into me. Just a little. He's enthralled by the sight if the glazed over look in his eyes is anything to go on. The slow stretch sends a moan right through me before he thrusts hard, causing the moan to get louder still. He's hard and fast and rough. The only part of my body touching the bed is my head and shoulders, and he fucks me like a beast. Sliding his hands up my back, and lifting my shoulders, he takes a nipple between his teeth and flicks it with his tongue. Then he bites and nips his way up my collar bone, pulling me up with him as he sits so I'm now straddling him, my bound wrists falling over the back of his head.

A feeling of being full and satisfied sweeps through me as I bounce on his cock, our hips never halting, and I cry out when he bites down on my neck and his fingers dig into my back. He nips at my flesh, licking it to soothe me afterward as he pounds into me faster.

The orgasm that was just out of my reach begins to build again. It starts in my toes and creeps up my legs, sending all those amazing tingles to my clit. The moan that escapes my throat is guttural, and it's matched by one from Nathaniel as he bites down again, his thrusts becoming more erratic. I can feel him everywhere, and I lean back slightly to push my nipple into his now open mouth.

He bites down on that too, and I shriek in pain that quickly becomes all-consuming pleasure, turning into wild screams of ecstasy each time he plunges into my pussy like a savage.

Then everything happens at once.

"Come all over my cock, Vixen." It's growled into my ear as he presses on, driving into me so hard I swear my coccyx will be bruised when we're done.

His words are all I need to come undone one more time. My release spreads through my entire body, at the same time as his cock pulses inside me and his thrusts get slower, more sensual. His large hands span my back, gently massaging everywhere he touches as we both breathe through our orgasm. The butt plug only enhances the sensations as my muscles contract around both that and Nathaniel's cock.

"Fucking heaven." His hot breath on my neck again sends a shiver down my spine, and he slowly lifts my arms over his head and lays me down, still seated inside me.

There are still some drops of wax on my chest and stomach, but I pay them no mind as he leans over me, placing the most gentle of kisses onto my lips before he pulls out. He takes his time releasing my wrists from his belt, kissing each of them and leaving tingles everywhere his lips touch.

"Bathroom?"

"Across the hall."

"Don't move."

He lifts himself to stand, pulling out some gray sweats from his duffel bag and climbing into them. I absolutely stare at his bare naked ass before the material covers it. Bending down over the bed, he holds one side of my face in his giant palm and kisses the shit out of me, his tongue dancing with mine before he starts to pull away, leaving me panting yet again.

My body is heavy with satisfaction, and the deep hum coming from Nathaniel only fans the flames that I really need to cool down. He leaves the room quietly, being mindful of everyone else in the house who are likely asleep by now. Although, with how loud we just were... maybe not.

My room is on the opposite end of the house from the other two. Petal was in the middle of decorating in here last time I visited—with strict instructions not to let Ev root through my drawers—and the wood landscape she painted on the wall opposite my bed is breathtaking. There was no time to really check it out before now, what with arriving, heading straight to the harvest, dealing with all the testosterone, and getting my brains fucked out, but now I can appreciate it in all its glory.

Petal doesn't really do a lot with her art, even though we all keep telling her she should. She's fucking amazing. The trees have so many layers and colors to them, and the depth of the moon in the top corner nearest my door is almost like looking at the real thing. The rest of the walls have been done in a pastel mint green—the color complimenting the mural perfectly—all mixed with my natural wood bedside tables, dresser, and bed. Add in my plush, deep green armchair in the corner, the color matching the window curtains, and this is a perfect space for me here.

Everest wanted me to always have a home with him and Petal, and since I'm buying the place anyway and spend so much time visiting, it was just sensible to have my own room.

Remembering the magnolia walls and all the times I've spent with Kai in this space, I close my eyes and take a deep breath. The bedroom door opening brings me back to now.

"Good girl. I found a clean washcloth in the bathroom."

The way he cleans the wax off me is soft and gentle, completely opposite to how he fucked me, but I'm beginning to understand there are many sides to Nathaniel Reed. He gently removes the butt plug, placing it on the cloth on the bedside table before pulling a clean, white T-shirt from his duffel bag and handing it to me.

"Put this on, Skittles."

I'm Skittles again now, and I'm not sure which I prefer. Skittles or Vixen. The fact he's taken the time to give me two nicknames makes me smile as I put on his T-shirt.

"Go and use the bathroom, I'll go and get us both a fresh glass of water from the kitchen." He pats my ass as I stand, and I squeal—quietly—resting a hand on my hip to look down at him sitting on my bed.

"Something to say?" He raises one of those sexy brows at me, a smile curling at his lips.

"Nope. But wait for me. Petal has a system with the filtered water she keeps in the fridge and I don't want you to use the wrong one. It'll start her whole day off wrong tomorrow." I shrug and grin, bending to kiss him lightly on the mouth before turning and leaving the room to go pee.

Finishing in the bathroom, I go back and let Nathaniel know I'm going to the kitchen. Of course he comes with me.

After pulling the right water jug out of the fridge, I refill our glasses, with Nathaniel standing behind me, his hands rubbing up and down my sides. Looking up, I catch our reflection in the window, and release a quiet moan at his gentle touch. We look damn good together.

"Bend over, my little vixen."

Vixen again? *I guess someone is ready for round two.*

The thought makes me smile. He must sense it, because his hands find their way to my bare skin, lifting his T-shirt up my back before pushing between my shoulder blades. Silently telling me to bend over.

I mean, it wouldn't be the first time I've ever done something like this in my brother's kitchen. My skin is still practically on fire from before, so I'm happy to do as he wants. Another orgasm will only make me sleep better.

Taking my earlobe between his teeth, he bites down gently, his hands cupping my ass tightly. Then his soft lips slowly make their way down my back until they reach the globes he's gripping. I close my eyes and throw my head back when his teeth find my clit, followed by a soft flicking of his tongue. Two fingers are added to the party, and he pushes them deep inside me, continuing his ministrations on my clit. Again, it's hard and fast, his aim is to make me come as quickly as possible.

And it doesn't take long at all. The man is a fucking clit wizard.

An orgasm is already building inside me, sending all those excruciatingly pleasurable tingles throughout my body as he continues to work his magic. Opening my eyes as my orgasm reaches its peak, they widen as I catch a reflection in the window that isn't myself. And Nathaniel is on his knees behind me, so it isn't him.

A breathy scream escapes my lips and all sensation becomes overwhelming for a few seconds, my brain is fuzzy and I almost want to cry or laugh hysterically, but all I can do is stare at Kai as I come. I don't know how much he saw, but he doesn't move until Nathaniel begins to stand again.

My stomach churns, and I'm not sure if it's just the after effects of my orgasm, or from the guilt I know I have no reason to feel.

It all happens so quickly before Kai disappears, and the creaking stairs are all that gives away his presence.

# Chapter Ten
## River

I've never had a boyfriend.

At least not as an adult. After I'd sneaked an unfortunate peak at Freya and Kai having sex in the trailer, my teenage-self thought the world had officially burned down, leaving me standing barefoot on smoldering hot coals.

Of course, I pretended I was fine. I put on the right smile and said the right things at the right time. Growing up surrounded by my brother and Kai meant that other boys never really showed an interest. We were always together. The four of us were inseparable until all I could ever see was a sixteen-year-old Kai on top of Freya whose legs circled his waist, pushing him down with the heels of her feet.

I'm not one to blame the woman in these situations. In fact, I believe women should own their sexuality. Revel in it. Live their orgasms to the fullest. But Freya knew what I felt for Kai. She always groaned when I brought him up, telling me to shut up about it and just do something instead.

That night, I'd decided that it was time to make things official. He was sixteen, I was almost fifteen, we could be boyfriend and girlfriend and live out our promises.

After all, it wouldn't have changed much except that I could hold his hand all the time and kiss him whenever I wanted.

Funny how the same night I told her I was putting on my big girl panties, she found herself lying underneath him, moaning.

The only reason I never blamed Kai was because he didn't know. That's it. Had Freya not known, I would have chalked it all up to teenage hormones gone wild.

But she knew.

She. Fucking. Knew.

So, yeah. I went through high school, dating a few guys here and there—one of whom braved the scathing glares coming from Kai and fucked me on his twin bed while his parents were away for the weekend—but never actually had an exclusive boyfriend.

Which brings me to my current predicament.

How do I know if I have a boyfriend? A real one? I suppose a conversation is necessary. Much like my contracts with my clients, we should be discussing our rules and conditions.

It's been a month since Samhain and I never thought I could have so many real orgasms without having to fake any of them. It took Nathaniel one night to find all the sweet spots that make my body sing with need.

I'm impressed.

The problem, you ask?

The fucking problem is that I'm a fucking prostitute. Fucking other men is literally my job. I have one client who likes me to fuck him with my strap-on until he practically passes out. His wife apparently has no idea he's fond of the prostate banging.

I don't understand why these men don't talk to their wives. So much shit could be resolved with a simple conversation. And she leaves because his kinks aren't her thing? Well, then, she leaves. It's also her right to not like said proclivities.

Let's take Elijah as an example.

We've been speaking on the phone, trying to set up the meeting with his wife. She agreed to coming a couple of weeks ago but according to Elijah, she didn't sound very convinced by his reasoning.

I'm at the apartment now, waiting on them to arrive as I arrange the different toys and props for her to take in. The bedroom area is separated from the kitchen by a dark sheer curtain I set up last week, so she didn't have to stumble in and come face to face with a St. Andrew's Cross from the get go.

From what I understand, Elijah was very cryptic with her. Practically begging her to just give him one last chance to explain himself, and one last chance to save their marriage.

I admire her courage for coming here. I know a lot of people prefer to keep their eyes closed and pretend everything is normal and socially acceptable in their lives.

Hell, so many of my clients pretend they're not cheating on their other halves or don't have specific needs in the bedroom. They come, do their thing, then walk out like they just had their cheat day and are going back to their regular diets.

It says a lot about a person who is willing to open the proverbial curtain and see what's behind it.

I hear their footsteps before the knock on my door. I'm dressed in black leather, this time with a see-through chemise that falls just to my hips, buttons open down the front. I'm in knee-high boots with the steel stiletto heels that give me the height I need to dominate Elijah's tall frame.

With a bright smile plastered on my face, I do my best to make myself look warm and welcoming for his wife as I open the door. In her position, I would hate me for being—for all intents and purposes—the other woman.

"Olivia, hi. It's great to meet you, finally." I extend my hand to shake hers and feel the awkward moment where she may very well refuse to touch me. Tentatively, she raises her hand and our palms connect with two shakes before letting go.

"Hi. I'm sorry, I'm really not sure what we're doing here so I'm a little out of my depth."

It's understandable but I can't let her build her walls up right from the beginning. She has to come into this with an open mind or else it won't work.

"I promise, we will explain everything to you. Please, come on in." I gesture to both her and Elijah, who is standing behind her, his face contorted in uncomfortable pain.

I want to tell him to grow some balls. Hell, his wife shows more just by being here.

"Hi Elijah, how are you?" I practically whisper to him because he looks like he might lose his fucking mind.

Hydration is always key, in any circumstance, so I've already prepared some glasses with fresh bottled water.

"Please, have a seat so we can discuss all the things."

Olivia is tall, her long legs are covered in denim and her cream-colored sweater exposes her right shoulder as it hangs perfectly off her breasts.

Every time you hear talk about the "girl next door", an image of Olivia should accompany the expression. Blond hair falls down her back and over her ample chest in long, thick strands people pay thousands of dollars to have planted on their scalps. Big blue eyes are staring at me, the picture of innocence and naïveté just pouring out of her.

But in those Bambi eyes, I see a spark. A curiosity that feeds her need to be here. To see what has been going on. To understand what her husband can't seem to explain.

And my respect for her grows tenfold.

"I don't know if Elijah has told you anything, but my name is Rose. Officially, I'm a life coach." She snorts at this and I can't help chuckling along with her.

"Is this what life coaches wear these days?" There's no animosity in her voice but the disbelief is clearly there.

Did I say she was naïve? I may have jumped to conclusions a little too fast there.

"You're right to be skeptical. But as far as Elijah is concerned, I want you to know that he and I have never touched." I push our contract toward her and open the pages to the exact paragraph that specifies that we are to never have skin on skin contact.

Giving Olivia a little bit of time to read through it, it's when her brows pinch together that I know she's reached the important part of the contract.

My duties.

"You hurt him?" Her voice is calm but low, like she's afraid of saying the words out loud.

"Yes." I leave no room for misinterpretation. "It's my job to inflict pain on him as he demands it."

Olivia turns to Elijah, who is imploring her with his devastated eyes not to walk out and shut the door on their forever.

"But…" Looking from him to me and then back to him, she asks, "why?"

A couple of weeks ago, I told Elijah that the most important thing would be to have her talk and ask as many questions as possible. The worst thing for her to do would be to shut herself off and leave.

The relief in his eyes when she turns her question to him makes me smile. Finally, his chest is rising and falling with each of his breaths. Breaths I'm pretty sure he stopped taking while he waited on her reaction.

Elijah doesn't answer right away, staring at her for a beat while I'm guessing he tries to collect his thoughts. He's had time to go over all of this in his mind but there's a difference between practicing the thoughts and actually putting them out into the universe.

While preparing the apartment, I set out some candles and crystals. Ironically, vanilla has a calming, familiar scent to it, yet vanilla is the exact opposite of what is about to go down in this apartment. As for crystals, I've set out a few different ones hoping they'll all converge. Between the rose quartz, topaz, and moonstone we should have love, forgiveness, and passion, among other energies.

As quietly as possible, I slide off my stool and extricate myself from the conversation just as Elijah begins his story. This is the explanation that she's been waiting to hear for months, over eighteen of them. I've heard bits and pieces, little crumbs of his trauma that he needed to share so I could understand his needs. Right now, this is a private moment for them but the studio is small and no matter where I go, I'll be able to hear him.

Sitting on the old leather chair, I face the high window, my back turned so as to give them intimacy.

"Do you remember that night the power went out while we were Skyping?" I suppose Olivia nods because he continues. "I wasn't able to contact you for a week after that because we'd been ambushed by militia in eastern Syria."

I zone out after that, going into my own thoughts, my mind wandering over to Nathaniel and the filthy things he likes to do to my body. To the meals he tries to prepare—failing most times—but insisting he likes to feed me.

"Rose?" I turn back to the couple and, with a quick glance at the clock, I realize twenty minutes have come and gone.

"Ah, yeah. Sorry." Standing, I resume my position on the stool.

I was hoping Olivia would hear the story and fall into his arms, begging him to rip up the divorce papers, but instead, she's looking at me with a million questions swimming in her eyes.

"Olivia has a few questions for you. Do you mind answering?" Crossing one leg over the other, I realize I'm in a defensive pose and try to go back and mirror Olivia's posture—leaning into her with my palms clasped together, eyes on her.

"Of course, as much as I can." They both nod at me and Olivia dives into her, apparently, long list of inquiries.

"Why you? I don't want to be rude, Rose, I just figure there are maybe... I don't know... better qualified experts?" She lets her words trail off and I'm going to assume she doesn't want to offend me. I smile, letting it reach my eyes because I really want them to get back together.

"Obviously, I'm not a therapist and..." I look over at Elijah and he nods, "Elijah has been talking to a professional so he can work on the psychological impact of his experience. To be honest, I'm not here to heal him, Olivia. My job is to do whatever he needs." She flinches, imperceptibly so, but I see it. It's written all over her face. She's hurt. Probably feeling betrayed.

"Olivia, these kinks aren't easy to share with people in general, and even harder to share with those we love the most when you've been told your entire life that it's wrong." Leaning in, I whisper like I'm telling her a secret. "He wanted to tell you everything, every time he was here, but the shame was more powerful than his need to come clean."

A lone tear falls from the corner of her eye and there, for the first time, she gives him an olive branch by sliding her hand over and clasping his fingers, squeezing so tightly I can see his skin turn white.

Elijah's breath gives out, he gasps like he's breathing for the first time in over a year and a half.

"Share with me, Eli."

A ball of warmth burns deep in my chest at the sight of them huddled together as she repeats, "Share with me. Trust me." He nods and it's my cue to walk over to the curtain, waiting on his permission to show her the things he'll need if she accepts to replace me.

It takes us almost thirty minutes to explain the different paraphernalia that he prefers for his pain. Except, this time he might actually be able to add a little pleasure to the pain, and that could be the beginning to his healing. She could be the balm to his wounds.

"Where would you like to start today, Elijah?" My back is turned as I open the box with his preferred leather floggers.

"The fifteen-inch beaded flogger." The impish grin he gives Olivia almost makes me chuckle. Those dead eyes he's had every session we've had are alight and alive, the transformation unmistakable.

A quick glance to Olivia, I don't miss the dart of her tongue over her lips, the way her eyes hone in on the box, an inquisitive glint shining in those bright blues.

Fleetingly, this moment gives me hope that maybe I could share my double life with Nathaniel; that maybe, he could be as understanding and accepting as Olivia; that maybe, together, we could find a solution, a different way of life.

Reaching to the back collar of his t-shirt, he pulls it up and over his head, folding it neatly on the end of the bed before walking over to the cross and facing away from us.

"The gist of it is that pain is a form of pleasure. Until now, it was only a punishment. We never worked on the pleasure part, he didn't want that."

Olivia nods, we've already talked about this.

"But you, you can give him both. He'll need your punishment, but he'll live for your encouragement, too." At her questioning eyes, I continue. "Tell him with your words that he's doing great. That you'll make him feel good. Tell him how you feel. Touch him, kiss his wounds. All of them. The welts and his internal scars."

"Can you show me?" Her voice is small, like she doesn't want to ask but needs to.

"Sure."

"Are you ready, Elijah?"

"Yes, ma'am."

"Good boy."

Swoosh. Slap. Grunt.

A pink stain instantly erupts between his shoulder blades, his body relaxing just a touch.

"Count."

"One."

Swoosh. Slap. Deep breath.

"Two."

I let the flogger tickle his skin from one shoulder to the other, then slide down his spine before another swoosh lands on his lower back.

"Three."

At ten I stop and without a word, hand the flogger to Olivia. Instead of timidly fumbling through the action, she takes her job seriously.

This time, she walks over to him and places the whole of her palm on his back, just below his neck, and slides her fingers between his shoulder blades before stepping back and printing her own mark on him.

"Eleven." The word comes out breathy, lust evident in his tone because he knows he's just hit a milestone. That shit would turn anyone on.

"No. You start over when it's me. You show me respect by calling me Mistress." It takes a lot to shock me, but holy fucking shit, she just brought this scene to a whole other level.

Looking over at me, she shrugs and, like it's supposed to mean something, she says, "Learned it from Sierra Simone."

Whatever gets her nipples hard.

I give her some direction, stepping up behind her to show her how to snap the wrist, how to hurt without wounding. How to turn this into something enjoyable for them both.

"Fuck." Elijah twists around, his face contorted in pain, but I know for a fact it has nothing to do with the flogger. He's taken so much worse from me.

"What's wrong?" I ask, placing a hand on Olivia's wrist and explaining that she needs to read his body language, needs to know when to give him more and when to hold back.

"I'm so fucking hard, it hurts." I grin and shake my head.

Olivia throws the flogger on the bed and walks up to Elijah, her fingers lightly skimming over the pink flesh, her mouth following the same path, one languorous kiss at a time, until she brings a hand to his nipple and pinches it enough to make him moan, bucking into nothingness.

"Do you still like my touch, Elijah?"

"Fuck... yes."

She pinches harder this time, enough to make him grunt and correct himself. "Yes, Mistress." In complete contradiction, she turns to me, her face the poster of innocence as she grins like she just won a panda at the county fair.

What the fuck dimension did I just fall into?

But then she's all business again and as her hand travels down his torso, she whispers something I can't hear into his neck and again, his hips buck in search of relief.

"I'll be in the kitchen if you need me." I speak softly, not wanting to break the moment but Olivia stops me.

"Rose?"

"Yeah?"

"I know you've done a lot for my husband but I need one more thing from you. We'll pay you, of course."

Frowning, I cock my head and nod for her to continue.

"You see, my husband once made a promise to me. He stood at the altar and promised to love me and cherish me forever. We were a team. I sat home, going to work every day and praying to God that he would come home from Syria." Now, she's taking her shirt off and mimicking

Elijah, she folds it and places it on top of his, like even their clothes are a team.

Then she's back behind her husband, untying his wrists, her lace-covered tits rubbing up against his back, probably causing him some burning. Elijah lets her do whatever she wants, her needs passing before his own.

"He used to be insatiable, like he couldn't get enough of me. Always touching me, fucking me in places that could be considered scandalous." She looks up at him, her eyes shimmering with unshed tears. "Do you remember your little brother's graduation?" Elijah's jaw is tense, probably trying to keep his own tears at bay.

"Yeah, of course, I do."

Olivia turns back to me, explaining. "He fucked me so hard I had bruises on my hips for three days. It was then we conceived our baby." They both choke on her words and I can only guess why because I know for a fact that they don't have any children.

"I'm sorry." My words are barely audible but I needed to say them.

"Then, when you came back from Syria, the man I loved, the man who was deep inside me and planted a little miracle, was gone. You. Were. Gone. And..." a sob escapes her pretty pouty mouth as she forces herself to say the rest.

"I thought you blamed me for the baby." Now her tears are free falling and she's not even bothering to wipe them off.

Elijah falls to his knees like she's just planted a knife deep into his heart. My throat is full of emotions and this isn't even my life.

"I thought it was my fault." She repeats her words like she needs him to understand that he's not the only one suffering.

"No, baby. No." Elijah is shaking his head, looking up at her imploringly.

I step back, really not understanding why I'm here.

"Rose," Olivia holds her hand back for me to take it. "Can you tie him back up, please?" Her voice is harder now, the mistress in her back with a vengeance. I'm intrigued, grinning like this is my favorite reality show.

In minutes, Elijah is back up on the cross, facing us this time.

"You almost lost me, you know that, right?" Of course he does, and I'm sure it's a rhetorical question because he doesn't answer.

"Did it ever occur to you that if you left me, I would find someone else? Have another man touching me?" She takes my hand and places it on her right tit and now I know exactly where she's going with this.

I've rarely had clients who have asked for a threesome, it's happened twice and it was in the beginning when I worked for Polly. It's hot, touching another woman. Her skin soft and her curves pliable under prying fingers.

This though? This is a lesson she wants to plant into his brain.

"My tits, you love my them, don't you, Eli?" She has my hand on her—pushing it down—wanting me to put on a show.

Stepping up behind her, I spread my stance and grab her hair, pulling her head to the side and running my nose along her neck while I massage her bra-covered breast. My eyes though, they stay on Elijah, watching his reaction. He's in pain, all right. His dick is so hard behind his jeans that I'm not sure if he'll be able to hold himself back.

Dropping my hand, Olivia walks over to him and stops just close enough to unbutton his jeans and grab his cock, her hold tight at the base, her eyes on him.

"Watch me, baby. Look at what you almost lost." She pumps him once, twice, then leans to the side and grabs a cock ring—she's a quick learner—and places it at the base of his dick before kissing the weeping head. His pre-cum is leaking steadily and I have no idea where he gets the strength to hold himself back.

"Good boy."

I watch as Olivia steps out of her jeans. Now in her lace lingerie, she drags down one strap then the other before exposing her tits and stepping up to her husband, whose lips are in a tight, straight line, in what I'm guessing is pretty much sexual agony.

I think she's got this whole Mistress thing down pat.

An hour later, we're standing outside my work studio, saying our goodbyes when I realize I'm so fucking horny that I might just go back inside and relieve myself.

But then I remember… I have a man who can do it for me.

"Good luck with everything," I tell them as Olivia gives me a prim hug. I mean, we're not best friends here, I was whipping her husband after all, but still, she thanks me for suggesting that she come and be a part of his healing.

I'm glad I did too, even though it's one less client on my roster.

Fuck, I need to stop losing my biggest revenues.

Walking them out, I make a last minute decision and text Nathaniel.

**Me**: Are you at the office?

Keeping my phone in hand, I take the stairs down to the 33rd Street subway, slaloming between businessmen and tourists. It's not until I tap my phone to pay the fare that I see Nathaniel's response.

**CAG**: Yes, I have one more patient to see and then I'm closing out. Dinner?

My phone says it's nearly seven-thirty which means I'll be there for closing. Perfect timing.

**Me**: Yes, I'll come pick you up.

**CAG**: I'll be waiting

As soon as the Six train arrives, I'm glad to see it's not as busy as the last one that slipped through before I could make it. A young woman tries to get her stroller onto the train but struggles. Now, my fellow New Yorkers may be rude, yet some guy doesn't even hesitate to help me pick up the wheels just enough to get the young woman on the train. We all smile at each other without really talking. Saying everything we need to say with a simple nod.

*Thanks.*

*No problem.*

It takes me about twenty-five minutes to get to Nathaniel's practice after changing at Union Square, jumping on the L train to First Avenue and walking the short distance to his office.

The light is still on and I can see his secretary packing up, smiling when I walk in.

"River! It's good to see you again." I met Shantelle a few weeks ago when Nathaniel asked me to come meet him for lunch. She's in her forties, I know, but fucking hell, she looks no older than twenty-five.

"Hey! How you doing?" I give her a quick hug as she turns off her desk light.

"I'm good. Go on in, he's waiting for you."

"Thanks, have a good night."

I don't waste time, heading straight to his closed office door, my body primed after having to wait all this time to be near him.

I knock, even though it's not necessary.

When he opens it, I'm blessed with his glorious grinning face. Still dressed in his white coat, his name tag placed right above his little pen pocket.

Nathaniel Reed.

Damn, even his name is sexy.

I cough, bringing my elbow to my mouth and pretending I'm feeling ill.

"I'm so sorry to be here so late, Doctor." And because he's kinky as fuck, he slides right into his role—all serious and professional—but just as turned on as I am.

"Hmm, come on in and I'll give you a quick exam."

Fuck yes. And by exam, I'm hoping he means his dick in my pussy.

I step inside and as soon as the latch clicks, he has me slammed against the wooden door, his mouth on mine, his tongue licking a hot path between my lips and slipping inside. Moaning into his mouth, I can't seem to get close enough to him and he somehow senses it because he quickly turns me to face the door, sinking his teeth into my earlobe and murmuring, "Jeans. Off."

Without a second's hesitation, I'm pushing the jeans I changed into before leaving the studio down to my ankles and using my feet to pull them off. Over my shoulder, I see him unzip his slacks as he walks over to his desk drawer and takes out a strip of condoms.

"Need a lot of those here, do you?" I smirk because damn, there's something hot about a man prepared to fuck at any time during the day.

We haven't discussed exclusivity and I won't lie to myself, but I hope I'm the only one he's giving orgasms to.

"Apparently so." Ripping the corner of the foil with his teeth, his eyes are on me like a predator about to destroy its prey.

"That ass is going to be the death of me, Vixen."

Hmm, I hope not.

"Maybe you should fuck it so you can tame it." His gaze slowly rises from my naked ass to my eyes over my shoulder, and the heat that's burning in his ocean blues makes my juices slide down my thighs. I'm so fucking ready it should be illegal.

"Oh, River. Trust me, I will fuck that ass and make it mine until sitting is impossible without thinking about me."

"Damn it, hurry the fuck up." Nathaniel freezes as he's sliding his condom on and without moving his head, he raises his gaze to mine, a single brow arched in disbelief at my sass.

I raise my own brow and shake my ass, distracting him long enough to have him slide his condom on in record time. Suddenly, he's pressing against me—five fingers curled around my hair and pulling my head back, giving him clear access—his mouth at my neck, his teeth nipping at my sensitive flesh.

"Good girls get to orgasm."

"And bad girls?"

In one smooth move he's inside me so deep, my words die on my tongue with a low groan.

"Bad girls get fucked, one tight hole at a time until they turn into good girls."

Pulling harder on my hair, he slams his free hand on the door and plunges into me over and over until I can't move, can barely stand, from the force of them.

"Goddamn, your pussy is..." Without finishing his phrase, he slides his hand to my jaw and turns my head, his mouth on mine, licking and kissing, his tongue pushing into my mouth and devouring every inch of me. With every thrust, I'm slammed into the door and with every push, Nathaniel swallows my cries.

Fuck, it's such a turn on. Everything about him makes me wet and needy.

When he's done feasting on my mouth, he brings his hand to my clit and with slow, determined circles, he primes me until I'm begging him to finish me.

"Nate, Nate, please, oh God, please."

Tap. Tap. Tap. Three times on my clit and I lose it. Taking in a deep breath, I scream his name as my body convulses with the feel of him still fucking me like he's on a mission to destroy me from the inside out.

"That's it, give it to me. Give me your screams, give me your moans." And I do.

With one final slam inside me, he gives me his orgasm and I give him a little bit more of my heart.

# Chapter Eleven

## River

Raoul's is one of my favorite restaurants in all of Manhattan. Situated in Soho, this place serves the best steak and the best burgers I've ever eaten. When I saw Polly's email last week confirming our dinner date would be here, I almost squealed with excitement.

The doors only opened five minutes ago, and I'm one of the first people inside, already seated at the bar and waiting for Polly and Frank to get here. She insisted we arrive as close to opening time as possible so we can be one of the lucky twelve to get Raoul's rare burgers this evening. With it being Black Friday, this place is going to get busy when people start rolling in from a day of shopping.

"Rose, darling!" Polly's lyrical voice that oozes class reaches my ears, and I turn from my stool to stand and greet her with a huge hug. She's wearing one of her favorite wigs today, a sleek black bob, and it really makes her beautiful cheekbones and blue eyes pop. The red satin blouse and black slacks she's wearing only add to her air of glamor.

Frank is hovering behind her, trying to blend in so he doesn't look like exactly what he is, her security. Blending in isn't his strong suit though, he's over six foot and bulked out to the max—not all of it muscle—and even when he's sitting, he looks like an adult at the kids' table.

"Have you ordered for us yet?" Placing her Chanel clutch bag on the bar, she takes a seat on the stool next to mine. "Frank, you can sit with us today. It's going to get busy in here, I'd like you close."

Polly's been through some shit, and she's well known around New York for what she does—a lot of the clients for her girls are politicians and those in high places—which is why she hired Frank. Embarrassed or betrayed wives, and husbands with a lot of money to spare, can often hold a grudge. Some of them even act on it. I'd only been one of Polly's girls for about three months when he started working for her. I don't think I remember the last time I saw her without him somewhere nearby.

"I have. The first three burgers of the night are ours, and the bartender is mixing our cocktails as we speak." Smoothing down my dark-gray pencil skirt, I sit back down as Frank takes a seat beside Polly. Silent as always.

"Oh good. Now that's out of the way, I actually have some business I'd like to discuss this evening, darling, and..." She pauses to take a sip of the Bloody Mannette cocktail in front of her before continuing. "Ooh, that's perfect. And I also wanted to apologize again for that client I sent you a few months ago." I struggle to contain my flinch at the mention of that horrific night and Polly's eyes turn softer as she speaks. "It turns out, he's done that to a couple of my other girls, and only one of them thought to tell me. Can you believe it?"

Her hands move around animatedly as she speaks. I'm always enthralled by her confidence and general attitude toward life; she seems so carefree. Although, I know it's taken a lot of blood, sweat, and tears for her to get to this point.

"Oh, wow. That's awful. Are the girls okay? Did any of them call the cops?" I have a feeling the dick in a box belonged to the cunt who scarred me—and Polly's other girls and whoever the fuck else fell victim to the sick piece of shit—but I'm asking anyway, because you never know. Maybe I should ask Polly about my *'gift'*.

"It has been dealt with. But Sally's still a little shaken up by it of course, and Ginger decided this profession wasn't for her anymore. I gave her a little bonus to help her along.

Sweet girl, she was. Reminded me a little of you in your younger days. Just a little less full of sass." Nudging my side with her elbow, she winks at me, a smirk playing on her lips, and I let loose a low chuckle.

"If Sally wants to talk, let her know I'm available. Ginger too, though I guess since she's decided she wants out, we won't be seeing her again."

"I will do, darling. That's very kind of you. And that little segway takes us to the business I wanted to discuss this evening."

Another sip of her cocktail. She's on some kind of mission to get out what she wants to say, she usually is when she has things on her mind. These cocktails are admittedly delicious. Just the right amount of vodka and tomato. I nod to let Polly know I'm listening.

"Okay, so, I've met someone…"

Before she can carry on, I'm interrupting, because wow!

"Oh my God, Polly! That's amazing! Who is he? And if he doesn't treat you well, let me know and I'll have his balls."

In all the years I've known Polly, never has she 'met someone' worthy of mentioning. She's concentrated on her girls and her business, so this is a huge development. To be honest, I thought she was fucking Frank at one point. Maybe she was, who knows?

Polly's laugh lights up her glorious face, it's infectious, and I can't help the beaming smile I'm giving her.

"Darling girl. I love you, thank you for saying that. But I have no worries. I've obviously researched the fuck out of him and he treats me like a queen."

"As he should."

"He's not what I wanted to discuss though." She pauses again, finishing off the last of her cocktail and letting the bartender know she'd like a top-up with just a tip of her head. I get the feeling what she's trying to explain is a little uncomfortable for her, which is unusual to say the least.

"Okay, how can I help, Polly?"

Turning to me, she is as serious as she's ever been.

"I'd like to take some time off so Charles and I can travel a little, just for a month. And I was wondering if you'd be able to keep an eye on my club for me? It won't be a lot of work, I already have Sheryl running things over there. All you'd need to do is be on hand if there are any problems and to pop in for a few surprise visits."

The fact that she's asking me to do this shows the amount of trust this woman has in me. And Polly having a boyfriend is almost beyond belief. But I'm excited for her, this is wonderful news.

"Of course. I'm honored you asked."

"Oh, sweet girl. You are and always have been my favorite. I see so much of myself in you, it's scary. Your determination is like no other, darling."

As she brings me in for a hug, I can feel emotion prickling at my eyes, but I'm not sad. Having this kind of respect from someone I hold in so much esteem is like having my parents tell me they're proud of me.

"Polly—"

"Darling, I don't need a thank you. Anyway, now that's out of the way, tell me, what's going on in the world of Rose?"

The burgers are placed on the bar in front of us before I can reply, and the smell is fucking divine. If I didn't already know the club Polly owned, I'd say this place could be hers; the artwork on the walls of nude female forms, the smokey-blues atmosphere, I'm pretty sure the bar hasn't been decorated for the last thirty-odd years, but it's perfection.

"How about you tell me about your new man first, Miss Polly. Don't think you're skipping over that whole thing. I saw the glint in your eyes when you mentioned his name."

I raise a brow at her before turning to pick up my burger. This is going to be messy, but oh-so-good.

Three hours—and an unmentionable number of cocktails—later, and we're ready to leave.

"How're you getting home, darling?" Polly loops her arm through mine as we exit the restaurant, which is now full of couples enjoying romantic meals.

"Cab." I grin at her widely.

"Oh no, Frank brought the car, you can come with us. We'll swing by your place first." She starts to pull at my arm, leading me over to a sleek silver Mercedes parked across the street. Frank is already standing by the car, holding the back door open for us. "Come on, darling. I won't take no for an answer. It might only be eight, but I'd feel better about seeing you home safely."

This isn't unusual for Polly after our dinner-dates. Which is the only reason I'm not arguing with her about this.

The smell of nicotine assaults my senses as I brush past Frank, and Polly passes me a bottle of water from inside the car to help my coughing. I fucking hate the smell of nicotine. One reason I've always avoided Frank, he stinks. If it was mixed with weed, that'd be completely different, weed gives tobacco a whole new and more bearable smell.

The ride home is quiet and comfortable, Polly is typing away on her phone with a huge smile on her face. I'm pretty sure she's talking with Charles.

She and Charles met when Polly's car was in for a service a few months ago, and from what Polly told me, they've been inseparable since then. He sounds like a fucking wet dream, and he looks like one too. If I had a daddy kink, I'd have been drooling all over the pictures Polly showed me.

It does make me wonder though, if Polly can have it all—her businesses and a boyfriend who understands—then why can't I? Have I been denying myself a relationship all this time for nothing?

I thought I was just following Polly's lead, if I'm honest with myself, but seeing her this happy is like seeing a whole new side of her. It makes me realize more is possible.

Maybe I didn't need to keep Kai at arm's length this whole time. Maybe I should let Nathaniel in completely. Maybe I can have it all, too.

Pulling up to my apartment, Polly gives me a huge hug and a kiss on the cheek. I know the bitch has just left her lipstick all over my face, which she finds highly hilarious. I just shake my head as I roll my eyes at her, and she giggles. Seriously, I've never seen this woman so happy.

The door is open before I reach for the handle, and Frank holds his hand out for me to take. I don't take it, because I'm surprised to see Nathaniel sitting on my stoop talking to Mr. Bobby.

"Rose, darling, that is one tasty morsel. I do hope he's yours?" She wags her brows like a teenager teasing their friends.

Is he mine? Can I claim him even though we haven't had *the talk*?

Can I claim anyone as mine without being fully honest with them about my double life? My secret?

Absolutely not, but I can pretend for now.

"Yes, he is."

"Ooh, you need to spill all the tea on our next dinner date, okay? Promise?"

I laugh. "Of course, Polly. Now go on home to your man, I've got my own to take care of."

As I turn to walk away, Frank grunts like a fucking grumpy villager from Minecraft before he slams the door closed and gets back behind the wheel.

"Nathaniel! What are you doing here?" I teeter over to them, my Louboutin's aren't made for running.

"Nice to see you too, Skittles."

His eye-crinkles become defined as that panty-melting smile crosses over his face before he reaches me and places a hand behind my neck to pull me into him for an equally panty-melting kiss. His tongue sweeps the seam of my lips, demanding entrance, and as soon as I open up, he's tasting every inch of my mouth. My hands find the back of his head, and I hold on, digging my fingertips into his once-styled hair and messing it up.

The last we saw each other was a couple of days ago in his office—he'd had to rush off for an emergency, after-hours patient—so I'm pouring everything into this kiss. Trying to let him know with just this touch of our mouths, that I'm thinking about more.

I'm still conflicted as fuck, but if I don't dive into something and start making some more grown-up decisions for myself, I'm going to be in limbo forever.

# Chapter Twelve

## River

Turns out, Nathaniel's visit had a purpose.

"Wait up!" I've stopped walking, my eyes narrowing on a big chunk of metal with wings and tiny wheels. "When you said 'go away for the weekend', I was expecting a nice drive in the country. This?" I point to the offending mode of transportation. "This is a fucking plane."

"It is." He's grinning down on me, his eyes full of mirth as I lose my shit.

Inspecting it a little closer, I see the Reed Industries logo on the tail of the plane—the light blue of the letters running along the side of the death trap all the way to the nose of the plane.

"I'm not getting on that thing." Nathaniel's grin disappears from his face, the worry clear as day.

"You're afraid of flying?" Bringing a hand to my face, he pushes the flyaway strands behind my ear but the wind just sweeps them back around.

"No. I'm afraid of spiders when they've grown to a certain size. I'm terrified of falling to my death in a great big ball of fire." He opens his mouth to say something but I cut him off immediately. "And do not give me that crap about planes are safer than cars blah blah blah." I cross my arms over my chest and I don't care that I feel and probably look like a petulant little brat.

"Okay, okay. But, if we don't catch that plane—that my mother graciously lent us—you'll never know what the surprise weekend was about." Oh, the little fucker. First, I don't want his mother to hate me for getting the plane all ready to go with the pilots and fuel and whatever else a plane needs but dammit, I want my surprise weekend.

Still...

"Nathaniel, I can't. I will curl up in a ball and cry." Reaching out for his hand, I squeeze to let him know it's no joke.

"Good thing I'm a doctor then, right?" Frowning, I release him and cock my head to the side as he opens his duffel bag and takes out a first aid kit.

"Are you going to blindfold me with gauze? I'll still be curled up—" He cuts me off with a laugh that hums throughout my entire body.

"No, Skittles. I have Ativan in here in case you want it. It'll reduce your anxiety." Side-eyeing him, I wonder if I can do this. I don't know where this irrational fear of flying comes from but it has ruled my entire life and the way I travel.

"Fine. But if I die, I will come back and haunt you everywhere, all the time." Grabbing my roller cases—two because I have no idea where we're going and a girl needs the right shoes for the right occasion—I walk ahead as though I were mad at him. I'm not, but I *am* scared shitless.

It's when he catches up to me and wraps an arm around my waist to stop me that my anxiety dies just a little. "There's a suite in the back of the plane where I plan to fuck the fear right out of you."

Okay, then. Carpe fucking Diem.

An hour later, I'm sipping on my third glass of champagne, feeling pretty fucking proud of myself for not needing to swallow down the Ativan before take-off—turns out the bubbly is just as effective.

"Can I get you anything else, sir?" The flight attendant—in all her blond hair, long legged glory—asks Nathaniel, sparing me a glance as an afterthought.

Now, I'm not a jealous woman, per se, but give me enough drinks and I can be petty as fuck. Imagine, I'm sitting in a private jet with a man whose hand is halfway up my thigh, his thumb rubbing circles, when she comes and practically spills her cleavage in his face. I get it, he's hot as fuck and any red-blooded woman—or man for that matter—would be blind not to get the sex tingles when around him.

What I don't get is the lack of respect, woman to woman.

"He's all good, I'll make sure of it." I pin her with my glare, a complete contradiction to the fake ass—maybe a little drunk too—smile on my face.

"That'll be all, Serena, thank you."

*That'll be all, Serena,* I mimic in my head in a tone that is in no way the same one Nathaniel used. The one in my mind is childish and ridiculous but I don't care.

Serena is barely out of sight before Nathaniel turns in his seat and the hand that was rubbing my thigh comes to the side of my face, his thumb at the corner of my mouth as he leans in and murmurs. "My dick is rock-hard right now. Never knew this little jealousy act could turn me on so fucking much." His lips are suddenly on mine, his tongue demanding entrance as he pries my lips open with a languorous lick.

Then we're both up and out of our seats, his hand clasping mine as he walks me down to the tail end of the plane, not bothering to slow down and making me keep up with him.

Hmm, I'm rather enjoying bossy Nathaniel Reed.

By the time we're inside the cabin, his jeans are unbuttoned, his cock standing proud in the opening as he slowly fists the base, sliding up and down as his eyes narrow on me.

"On your knees," I can see the strain in his forearms, the veins pumping blood up and down with every one of his movements. I don't hesitate, I'm kneeling in front of him but I don't open my mouth like a good little slut. I wait for him to ask. Nicely.

Which he absolutely does not.

"Mouth open, tits out." I grin up at him, unbuttoning my shirt just enough to give him my cleavage, like the flight attendant. It's the cock of my head and the raise of my brow that makes him lose his control, I think.

Leaning down, he grabs both sides of my shirt and pulls hard enough to have my buttons flying across the carpeted floor of the plane.

"Well, that's going to be a bitch to pick up." I don't really give a fuck, I have three other shirts like this in my suitcase. Besides, it'll give big boob Serena a lot to think about as she's on her hands and knees picking up the buttons he ripped off of me. Cunt.

"Maybe I'll have you pick them up with your smart mouth while I fuck you from behind? Think that'll convince you that I don't look at other women while I'm with you?" He's got one finger under my chin while his other hand is stroking his cock, bringing it closer and closer to my mouth.

"We never said anything about being exclusive." This is where shit gets tricky. I can't promise him anything, which means I may have to take a chance on the truth.

The storm that begins to rumble in his eyes makes me pause. It's not anger, it's something more, something possessive.

"No, we didn't. You have something you need to share?" His usually open expression is clouded, like he's really expecting me to air out my deepest, darkest secrets.

Goddammit.

"I'm trying to share my body with you but you keep talking and delaying, so..." I open my mouth and stick my tongue out like I'm a baby bird waiting for her meal.

Making himself comfortable in the seat, he sticks his thumb in my mouth and gives me a bossy, "Suck." Making a big show of licking and biting and sucking on his thumb, I tense at his next words but remind myself that I'm not fucking anyone else at this moment so, technically, I'm not in the wrong.

"I don't fucking share, River. You get that, right? So if you have anything to tell me, now's the time."

And with that little nugget, he pushes his dick in my mouth and buries his hands in my hair, digging his fingers into my scalp as he pushes right to the back of my throat.

I'm a pro at this. Quite literally, so I don't choke but if my job has taught me one thing, it's that men like to think their cocks are choking the life out of their partners. They like to see the struggle, have the feeling they're so big that we can't breathe. They like to see the tears falling from the fight for air.

So I give him the show he deserves.

Until I don't have to anymore. Until he's so far deep in my throat that I'm afraid I might actually gag. He gets his tears, his thumbs coming up and rubbing them away like it's a gift I'm presenting him on a silver platter.

"You're stunning when you're crying."

Fuck. I'm so wet right now, I might have to sink my hand into my jeans and get myself off while he fucks my mouth without any civility.

It's so fucking hot, I can barely stand it.

"Don't do it, Vixen." Dammit.

Pulling out of my mouth, he brings me to my feet and kisses me like he didn't just have his dick down my throat. I love that it doesn't bother him. I'm so used to men with their particulars that I forgot what it's like to be with someone for the pure pleasure of it.

For *my* pleasure.

The plane dips with turbulence and I feel my stomach drop with the fear of crashing.

"Shh, you're okay. Get on the bed." His words are orders but the fact that he's actually taking me there shows me his concerned side.

Then on the bed, he's practically ripping my clothes off, his nostrils flaring with the lust I can clearly see in his eyes as they roam over every inch of me.

Gripping both of my wrists in his one hand, he places them above my head as he covers my body with his—still clothed. His mouth starts at mine, travels down my neck and makes its way to my chest and nipples. With licks and bites, he sucks until I'm pushing up toward his mouth and silently begging for him to take more. Give more.

Continuing a trail down my stomach, he releases my wrists to clasp the back of my thighs and push them up and over his shoulders, burying his face between my legs.

"Goddamn." Then his mouth is kissing my cunt, licking a path from bottom to clit where he flicks his tongue enough to make me squirm, make me grab the comforter to avoid digging my nails into the back of his head. I'm so fucking close that I have to hold myself back when he pushes two fingers inside my pussy—so wet and needy—before he sucks on my clit and circles it with his tongue at the same time.

I lose the battle when he curls his fingers and applies the perfect amount of pressure right where I need him.

"Oh, fuck, fuck, fuck!" I have no control over my body, I'm a writhing, screaming mess as I take his head in my palm and push him into me, rubbing his mouth on my cunt while I come all over his gorgeous face. The fingers of his free hand are digging so deep into my thigh that I briefly think he's going to leave a mark.

And I'm okay with that.

My arms fall to the mattress as I feel him rise from between my thighs. Opening my eyes, I watch him as he runs his tongue over his mouth, sucking on his bottom lip like he can't get enough of my taste. It's a fucking turn on when a man gets hard from your cum. It's the best compliment you can get.

Reaching back, he grabs his shirt and pulls it over his head before pushing down his jeans, not wasting any time as he slams into me, grunting when his dick slides easily all the way to the hilt.

"Fuck, River." I grin, groggily, like I'm drunk on him.

"Yeah. I know." We kiss the entire time he fucks me, tongues battling at the same rhythm as his hard pumps, sweat forming on our chests, wet sounds ringing around the cabin as he grunts with every thrust, tearing unsolicited moans from between my lips.

I scream his name as he buries himself deep inside me, his jaw tight, his eyes fixed on me. His mouth whispering a distinct, "Fuck."

"Did we forget the condom?" I'm not concerned about myself, I get tested regularly and take birth control. But this isn't something I can afford to forget.

"I put one on, don't worry. You were too out of it to notice." He grins, kisses me one last time before sliding out and—true to his word—discards the condom in the wastebasket.

"Guess you didn't notice the turbulence either, did you?" Oh, he's so fucking proud of himself.

"No, I thought that was us."

We end up landing in Buffalo and taking a chauffeured car into Niagara Falls. As decreed by Nathaniel, this is a no-phones weekend. Two days just for us, without distractions, only orgasms.

The American side is mostly quiet and nature oriented and I liked the thought of hanging out with trees and the water, but Nathaniel had other ideas.

"We're going to Canada?" I'm bouncing in the seat because I've heard great things about both Canadians and their side of the Falls. As a New Yorker I'm supposed to scoff at the idea that anything is better than ours. I mean, pizza? Check. Hot dogs? Check. Baseball? Fucking check.

Which means I get to investigate what all the hype is about.

"We are. You ever been?" Nathaniel leans forward toward the compartment that conceals a tiny fridge and gets two waters out.

I was able to get myself together after he fucked the fear of flying out of me, but my legs still feel like jelly and I'm irrationally parched.

"Nope." I thank him for the water, drinking half of it in one go.

"You're going to love the hotel."

It takes a while to cross the border, our arrival time on a Friday isn't ideal, but we're not in any hurry. The border patrol smiles and wishes us a great time in Canada, and I smile like a kid about to go to Disney World for the first time. Side note, my parents were ferociously opposed to all things Mickey Mouse, so no... I've never been there either.

As we cross the bridge, I lean over Nathaniel to see the emblematic cascade and I fall silent, in awe of its beauty.

"That's our hotel, right there." He points to the closest tall building to the actual Falls and my grin just gets bigger.

"You are so getting laid tonight." As if it wasn't already a given but hey, consent and all that jazz.

Friday night we walk around the town, hand in hand, just taking everything in. The place is like a kid's paradise. The rides, the candy shop, the huge arcades, the chocolate factory—I may have bought a ton for Petal and Everest and yes, for Kai as well.

My life has been a series of responsibilities that I have taken seriously from the day my parents died. I have been on top of my game, taking care of my brother and myself. This trip reminded me that I'm only twenty-six and I have the right to lay back and have fun.

We spend too long outside—and the end of November in Canada is fucking freezing next to the wind caused by the waterfall—but it is impossible to walk away from the sight. The contrast between the calm water that flows harmlessly to the edge of the falls, and the storm of mist and noise as it plummets over the edge and drops into the basin a hundred feet below takes my breath away. It's impossible to be indifferent to this natural wonder.

"I knew it was beautiful, but I can't look away. It's just... absolutely stunning." I'm cuddled in the warm embrace of Nathaniel's arms—my back to his front—our gloved hands wrapped around each other as we take in the scenery and listen to the other tourists oohing and ahhing.

"I used to think the same thing." I look up at him without moving my body, intrigued.

"Used to? Like, not anymore?" Clearly, he's lost his mind.

"Not until I saw you next to it. Now, compared to you, it's subpar." It takes me a moment to register the cheesy line he just dared say out loud.

"You get laid with those lines?" I'm laughing, pulling him tighter against me.

His mouth falls to my ear and my whole body reacts instantly. "The entire hotel floor is going to know just how many times."

Needless to say, the rest of the night was spent with his fingers, tongue, and cock making me come until I passed out.

The next day we do all the tourist must-do's, including the Hard Rock Café, and when we return to the hotel, he tells me to wear something outdoorsy. Of course, I think of Timbs but he put a veto to that, telling me the last thing we need is a broken ankle.

I pout, he ignores me.

Then he fucks the pout right off my face.

"When you were a kid, did you play hide and seek?" We've been walking for an hour along the water and then a little further up until we're pretty much in a secluded area surrounded by trees. It's brisk out but, as he repeated many times, the walk will make the cold seem welcomed. I don't know about that but it feels great to be outside the city.

"Sure, of course. With Everest and Kai mainly. Sometimes with Freya, too, but she couldn't see the point in hiding so she'd just sit behind a tree." I shrug at the memory and feel something has changed. The charge in the air is electrified, somehow. I stop walking when I notice Nathaniel isn't next to me anymore.

"What's going on?" Without a word, he stalks me, his blue eyes bright with the cold but sunny day. His mouth has a dangerous smile to it, like a predator sizing up its prey. When he reaches me again, he looks to the woods just feet away before his gaze swings back to me.

"I'm going to give you a thirty second head start. The longer it takes me to find you, the harder I'll make you come." I laugh at the ridiculous notion that I would run for any man when his palm suddenly covers my mouth and nose, his eyes dark with promise and a grin so dangerous a tiny shiver runs down my spine.

"River?"

I can't talk so I just nod like a mindless doll.

"Run."

The tone of his voice is a shot of lust that runs through my entire body. I don't think, I don't argue. I don't even know where the fuck I'm going, but just follow my instincts. It doesn't take long to reach the small forest, leaves crackling with every step I take, branches attacking me from above as they hang—naked—from the maple trees. I look left, then right, knowing damn well he's not far away. His legs are longer, stronger than mine, but I'll be damned if I let him win. It's then I see a thick trunk with low enough branches that I can climb them and hide. So I do, all the while trying to calm my breathing down so he can't hear me as I huddle in the small patches where leaves are still hanging on for dear life.

The sweet scent of the damp leaves reminds me so much of my childhood that I ache a little for my younger years. I can't believe I'm doing this. Running and playing some kind of adult version of hide and seek is thrilling and fun. I haven't felt this carefree since before my parents died. Before I watched as the life behind their eyes faded away.

I haven't felt this alive since that fateful night.

It takes him ten minutes to catch up to me and the only reason it took him that long was because I climbed the tree, hoping he wouldn't see me.

He *definitely* saw me.

Jumping down, I take off running, avoiding the frozen patches of leaves that litter the ground and praying I won't break something on my quest to win a stupid game.

The next thing I know, I'm tackled to the ground from behind just as we hit a pile of leaves, breaking my fall nicely. I kick and scream but Nathaniel is on my back, his hand at my mouth, his lips at my ear.

"Gotcha, little vixen." He's wearing sweats, so there's no sound warning me that he's pushing them down before he grabs the back of my yoga pants, along with my panties. In one move, making any porn star proud, I hear the ripping of foil just before he thrusts inside me so hard my breath catches in the cold air.

"Fuck, you're so hot inside. You're fucking perfect." I push my ass back into him, barely aware that anyone could walk by or catch us fucking in the middle of the woods.

I'm breathing hard into his hand, the urge to bite him is strong but instead, I curl my fingers into the leaves and meet him thrust for thrust.

It's hard and it's fast, his movements jerky and needy, his free hand sliding beneath me and into the front of my yoga pants to pinch and circle my clit.

My breaths are heavy, my pants probably loud enough to be heard by passersby, but in this moment I don't give a fuck.

"Fuck, the thrill of chasing you down, Vixen, made my dick so fucking hard." God yes, I'm so wet I can hear myself sucking his dick in every time he slams into me.

It's not long before the fear of getting caught makes my orgasm burst from deep inside me.

"That's it, give it to me."

And I do.

Long and fucking hard.

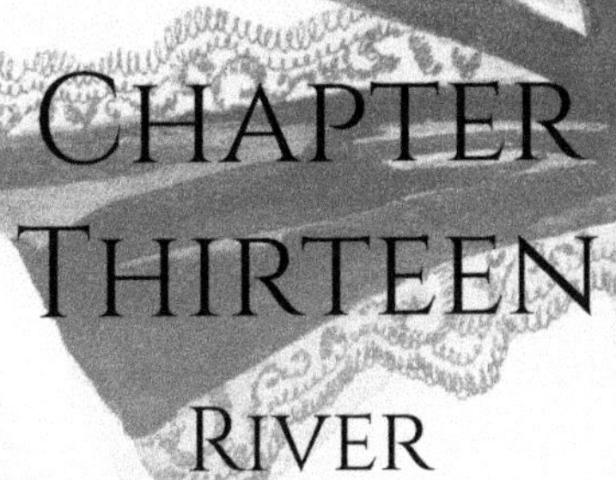

# Chapter Thirteen

## River

The Ativan wasn't needed again on the plane home, though the three orgasms definitely helped.

"Here's your phone, Skittles." Nathaniel hands me my cell after pulling it from the small zipped section of his bag as we sit in the back of the car, already turning his own on and checking his messages.

This is the thing with Nathaniel, in the time we've spent together, we've had a great time—and the sex is fucking fantastic—but there comes a point when he's back on his phone. Texting or calling, all work related. It just feels like he has a timer set for how long he can spend focused on me, and when he's done, he's back to the grind.

Although, with that thought, comes the gratitude for his time spent working. It means less questions about my own unusual hours. I'm not saying I haven't rearranged a client or two over the last month so I can spend the night with Nathaniel, but, whatever.

Work being a pain in the ass—for both of us—is one of the reasons I agreed to the whole phones-being-off thing in the first place. I thought having the whole weekend together, just the two of us, was going to be really special, and it was, but now I have this strange urge for post-sex intimacy, like a cuddle or some shit. Except it's post-fuck-fest-weekend.

Maybe I'm expecting too much. He is pretty fucking perfect. And did I mention the orgasms?

With the early afternoon sun streaming through the half-open window, my phone starts pinging in my hand after it comes to life.

"Someone's popular." Nathaniel raises a brow and looks at me out of the corner of his eye as he types something on his phone.

"Well, you know me. High in demand." Now, I'm not normally one for auras, but I swear to fuck I saw Nathaniel's change when I said that. It happened too quickly to really tell, and I'm not Petal, so maybe I'm just imagining things and my lame-ass joke that hit too close to home wasn't actually as funny out loud as it was in my head.

There are fifty-seven missed calls from Petal, forty-eight from Kai, twenty voicemail messages and seventy-four unread texts… all on my personal phone—I left my work phone at my apartment.

Holy fuck, why so many?

The first eight unread messages are from Petal.

**Petal:** I don't know what to do. He won't wake up.

**Petal:** There's blood everywhere.

**Petal:** The ambulance is on the way.

**Petal:** River? Where are you?

**Petal:** Please pick up the phone!!!

**Petal:** River??!!!

**Petal:** The ambulance is here.

**Petal:** River!! Please pick up!!

No no no no no!

Fuuuck.

I'm shaking, physically unable to stop myself from doing so. Do I want to read anymore? I need to call her. One of Kai's unread messages catches my eye.

**Kai:** Call me back, Psyche. I love you.

My hands fly to my face with my cell on my knees and I just stare at the screen.

"River? What's wrong?" Nathaniel places a hand on the back of my neck and begins to rub slow circles with his fingers and thumb.

Shit. *Pull it together, River.*

"I don't know. I need to call Petal and Kai back. I think something's wrong with Ev."

"Your brother?"

"Yeah." I know I'm mumbling as I pick up my phone and dial Petal, there's no point in listening to the voicemails. And something must be really fucking bad if Kai is telling me he loves me.

Petal answers on the first ring.

"Oh my Goddess, River! It all happened so fast. Where have you been?" She's crying, and for the twenty-millionth time this fucking year, I feel tears prickle at my own eyes.

"Petal, calm down, honey. Tell me what's going on." I'm calm, my voice as steady as I'm able to keep it, which is actually pretty fucking impressive and I'm proud of myself. Petal doesn't need me to break down with her.

"Oh, Riv, there was blood everywhere, and he wouldn't wake up, and he was just lying there, and, oh Riv! Please tell me you're on your way?"

I've never heard Petal sound so scared in all the time I've known her. It's getting harder by the second to stay calm and strong. My heart is sinking into the pits of darkness and I don't think it'll ever come back if this conversation goes where I fear it might.

"Okay, Pet. I'll be there as soon as possible, I have the address you texted. Is Ev awake now?" I should give myself a fucking medal for how calm I sound on the outside right now.

"He woke up in the ambulance, concussion, but the doctor said he'll be okay. He's getting an x-ray right now because they think he's broken some bones. And Riv, I've never been so scared in my whole existence." Her cries have softened to hiccupping sobs, and I'm going to give that girl the biggest squeeze when I see her. The relief I feel at knowing my baby brother is awake and 'okay' makes my entire body slump in the soft leather seat.

"Are you with anyone?"

"Yes, Kai's here. He's been sharing his energy with me or I really would have fallen apart by now, Riv. Honestly, I don't know what I'd do without my Bear."

"Well, it sounds like we're lucky you won't have to find out any time soon. I'll be there as soon as possible and it'll be like hug-city, okay, Pet?"

She's a lot calmer now, her breaths still catching on a tear-filled hiccup every now and then, but it's a lot less than when she answered the phone.

Nathaniel is watching me intently the whole time I'm on the call, patiently waiting for me to finish with a concerned look on his face. We talk for a few more minutes, Petal able to explain what happened once she's a little calmer, and I hang up with reassurances that I'll be there with some abalone and lapis lazuli crystals as soon as I can.

Staring at the phone in my hands, I'm silent as I try to absorb all the information I've just been given.

"Skittles…? River? Is everything okay?"

It's then I realize his hand is still on the back of my neck, the sensations and feeling in my body finally coming back to me as my terror eases. With the way the universe has been throwing shit at me recently, I expected the worst when I called Petal. For the first time in a long time, I took a weekend for myself. Taking advantage of the freedom to just be happy, without a care in the world.

I was River.

Not Rose the escort, not protector and big sister, not the complicated best friend.

Just River.

And then the world stopped moving around me. With a few text messages, I was transported back to the worst day of my life. The day I saw my parents die right in front of me.

Maybe I shouldn't have gone this weekend.

With a deep breath, I shake away the guilt, because everything will be fine. It's all good. The worst didn't happen, and I am allowed to live my life. But what if...

"I need to get to Staten Island as soon as I'm home. Ev's in the hospital with a concussion and possible broken bones. So it's all a bit fucked, and Petal is distraught, even though he's going to be okay because she thought the worst when she found him at the bottom of the tree." I pause to breathe, trying to process it all, rubbing at my forehead with my fingertips in frustration and relief. "Turns out, the branch wasn't as strong as he thought it was."

"Shit. I'm glad he's okay. How are you doing?"

*How am I doing?*

"I'm good. I think. Sorry to put a downer on the weekend." Knowing Ev will be okay has brought a sense of relief like I never knew I needed.

"Are you kidding? No, of course not. We'll stop off at your apartment for whatever you need, then go straight to Staten Island together."

He moves his hand from the back of my neck, wraps it over my shoulder, and pulls me closer. The warm, comforting smell of him helps to calm my nerves.

"What about your patients? I'm going to be there for a few days, you can't miss work for that long, can you?"

I'm almost hopeful that he actually can.

"No. I'll have to come back on the last ferry tonight or early in the morning. But I want to be there for you."

"Really, you don't need to come. He's awake, it's not serious. I'm a big girl." The disappointment clawing its way up my insides needs to back the fuck off, but I smile anyway. We're not in a relationship, and he has an important job. It's selfish of me to expect what he's never promised. Especially when I can't give him my full self either.

Relaxing into him, I close my eyes and allow my thoughts to wander for a few minutes. Or maybe more than that, as before long, Nathaniel is gently whispering into my ear.

"Wake up, Skittles, we're here. Go and get your things together."

Opening my eyes, I look out the window to see my apartment building.

"I'll wait in the car for you, because if I come in there, it'll take a lot longer than a few minutes."

Only one thing can make me turn an offer like that down.

My family.

So, I guess he's waiting in the car.

"Oh, River! I'm so glad you're here. I'm a mess, and they're still testing and scanning him. I haven't seen him for two hours! And Goddess only knows what kind of radiation all of those scans are doing to him."

*Thank fuck I made sure Ev and Petal got top rate medical insurance in place a few years ago, or this would've been an expensive visit.*

Petal is waving her hands around animatedly as she speaks, and she is clearly not herself right now.

"Come here, Pet." Opening my arms wide, I bring her in for a hug. A real hug. The kind Petal is always so willing to give and experience with everyone else. The kind she really needs. I hold her close to me for a few minutes, our arms wrapped fully around each other in an act of love and understanding.

Nathaniel is hovering behind me in the waiting room. It's a little awkward that he came, considering he's leaving again soon, but it's actually really sweet that he has made the effort. Even if I'm feeling a little selfish.

"Excuse me, Mrs. Fox?" The man standing in the doorway could be mistaken for George Clooney, with a spattering of gray hair at his temples and a kind smile on his tanned face.

Both Petal and I answer as she turns to face him before I roll my eyes at myself. He didn't mean me, and I'm not a Mrs.

"Yes? That's me. Is everything okay?"

Even though she knows he's out of the woods with his injuries, the panic in her tone is evident with a slight wobble of her voice and the widening of her eyes. She looked doll-like before, but with her eyes open this wide, all she needs is pigtails and freckles.

"Yes, of course. Mr. Fox is back in his room and allowed visitors again. His leg has been put in a cast, and he will need to stay off it for a few weeks. His femur is broken and needs around three to six months healing time. We're hoping more toward the lower end of that since it was a clean break. And we will need to assess if he will need physical therapy when we can see how it's healing."

"Okay, can we see him now, please?"

Nathaniel has moved behind me as Petal speaks with the doctor, wrapping an arm around my waist and pulling me into him in a protective gesture that kinda makes me swoony.

"Yes, if you could follow me. Will the gentleman that was here earlier be coming back?"

Speak of the devil and he shall appear. Kai walks in behind the doctor, three coffees in hand, and he pauses—ever so slightly—when he sees me standing with Nathaniel. It's only miniscule, but I know him.

"I'm here, I was just getting coffee. Everything okay, doc?"

"Everything is fine, sir. I've explained a little bit to Mrs. Fox, and we'll go over the rest shortly. But I get the feeling Mrs. Fox is eager to see her husband, and we have some new visitors, so, shall we?" Doctor Fraizer, as his name tag tells us, turns to leave, expecting us all to follow as he leads the way.

Petal claps her hands together and the beaming smile on her face is full of excitement at seeing Ev again. It sends a warm feeling through me to know my brother is loved so much. Kai hands Petal a coffee, the smell making her nose scrunch up like a mouse.

"I don't know why you bought me this obscenity, Kai. The coffee in those machines is not organic in any way. But thank you for being so thoughtful." She puts it on the small table by the door and gives him a kiss on the cheek before following the doctor. Leaving the three of us in the room. Alone.

Fun times.

"Kai." Nathaniel's voice rumbles through me, and I see him from the corner of my eye nod his head in greeting. His arm still wrapped tightly around my waist.

"Nathaniel." Kai nods his own head in that manly way they do, pretending they respect each other. I know it's bullshit.

Nathaniel and I haven't spoken about Kai since Samhain, and Kai and I haven't spoken about Nathaniel.

I haven't done it intentionally, and I'm not hiding my friendship with Kai or my whatever the fuck with Nathaniel. It's just that in the few short phone calls I've had with Kai over the last month, we've been working on just being friends again, and it's been amazing. I'm also positive Nathaniel doesn't want to talk about my best friend-slash-ex fuck buddy.

"Come on, let's go see Ev."

It's me who takes charge, the weird stand-off between the guys is too much right now. The testosterone is practically choking me, and not in a fun way.

On our way to my brother's room, I grab Petal's discarded coffee and hand it to Nathaniel—he needs it more than any of us—all the while ignoring Kai's ridiculous growl of disapproval.

Waste not, want not.

"I'm going to stay here with Ev. Can you go back to our place, please, River? The chickens need feeding and I didn't have time to prepare them for us not being there. I don't want them to get lonely."

Petal is pleading, her big brown eyes could pass for one of those cute puppies in a cartoon as she bats them at me. Visiting hours are over for the rest of us, but the doc is allowing Petal to stay since Ev is in a private room.

"Yes, of course. Do you want me to bring you both some fresh clothes in the morning?"

"I can give you a lift on my way home, Riv."

Nathaniel has been plastered to my side the whole time we've been in Ev's room, and his hold tightens on my shoulder when Kai offers me a lift.

"Oh that would be wonderful. Some clean underwear and some toiletries please. You're such an angel."

"Ew, Pet, baby. My sister doesn't need to be touching my underwear. I'll go commando until we get home, thanks."

Ev looks like shit. A small bruise on his forehead, and his leg raised and in a cast, but he's alive. And for that, I'm thankful.

"Yeah, I'm with Ev. I know what a dirty fuck he is, so there's no way she should be touching his tighty-whities. We'll bring everything else though. Okay?"

"They're comfortable, dammit." I hear my brother mumble and the relief that they're bantering like any normal day makes the weight on my shoulders lift just a fraction.

We're all smiling, laughing at Ev's dirty underwear, apart from Nathaniel. He's been silently stoic and unmoving, which is a little disappointing because I thought he was really going to make an effort. He is the one who insisted on coming with me.

"I can take you to your brother's before I catch the ferry." It's whispered in my ear, and with the others talking among themselves, they don't realize he's finally spoken. His breath tickles at my neck, and I turn into him, brushing my lips against his. I can feel his body relax at the gesture. Maybe he just needed some reassurance.

"You have to catch a cab, it seems silly to pay the extra fare to take me to Ev's and then you to the Ferry. It's literally on the way home for Kai."

I get his trepidation about me being alone with Kai, but he just sees him as an ex rather than my best friend. Which I know is my fault for not explaining it properly, but as I said, it never came up. I'm pretty sure this makes me a bit of a bitch, but I'm really not trying to be. There will come a time when Nathaniel understands what Kai is to me, and that he has nothing to worry about. He's engaged for fuck's sake.

I mean, if we're getting technical here, then Kai is the least of his worries.

"Look, is there something I need to worry about? Is Kai going to be an issue?"

Wow, that escalated. The way he's speaking makes it sound like we're a lot more serious than dating. Maybe he wouldn't be as cool with my profession as Polly's new man is.

"No! Kai is our best friend, Ev and I have known him our entire lives. Plus, he's engaged to Freya. And that's it."

I've turned to face him now, both his hands at my waist as we speak within our own little bubble in the corner of the room.

"I don't trust him."

I get that too. But if he's nothing else, Kai has always been faithful. He would never cheat on Freya.

"Well, you just have to trust me then, don't you?"

His right eye twitches as I speak, like he's trying to hold off from telling me he doesn't trust me, but he seems to make a decision in that same moment.

"Okay. My cab's out front, so I'm going now. Call me when you get back."

Then he kisses the ever-living shit out of me. His tongue licking at the seam of my lips to force them open for him as he explores my mouth to the sounds of oohs from Petal, and fake throwing up noises from Ev. Kai remains silent.

Fuck this tension bullshit.

# Chapter Fourteen

## River

After Kai dropped me off two days ago—and after I insisted he go home rather than staying to keep me company—I spent the evening putting my things away before setting up the living room couch for my brother's arrival; from blankets to pillows, to tables and magazines. They don't have a television but they have board games, which I put in the corner in case he gets bored and needs some family time. It's the very reason he's whining now while Petal is trying to give him kisses at an awkward angle to avoid hurting him.

"But Kai doesn't know anything about harvesting and planting. Hell, he can't keep a plant alive to save his fucking life."

Kai, who's sitting in the chair flipping through one of Ev's organic agriculture magazines, just flips him off without even raising his gaze.

"Oh, Bear, you just need to tell him what to do and he'll do it. And me, too." Petal looks up at me expectantly, not sure if I'm staying or not.

"Yeah, and me too, little brother. I know a few things about that... stuff." I know nothing except when in doubt, prune it all down and watch it grow again.

Ev and Kai both snort like I've just said the most ridiculous thing in the history of the Fox family.

"I do!" I'm defensive, which is its own brand of admission that they're right.

"Remember that time she got an ivy plant for her room, swore she'd care for it like it was a pet?" Kai's holding down a corner of the magazine so he can look at Ev, mirth dancing in his eyes.

"Dude, of course I remember. Who kills a vine? Those things are invincible." Ev's now laughing as Petal tries to fuss over him, making sure he's comfortable. Must be doing fine if he's capable of roasting me.

"I was twelve. You two can fuck right off."

They all laugh at my indignation and for the first time, I'm the one acting like a brat.

Despite all of the ribbing, this feels so right. I'm with my family, laughing and helping each other out like always. Looking over at Kai, his smile brightens his whole face and I know, without a doubt, that he's feeling it too. This warmth, this positive energy.

Then Petal kills it with a simple question.

"Where's Freya?" Kai's smile drops instantly, his gaze flitting to me before going back to whatever is so fascinating in his magazine.

"She's started making her own skin care products, needed to get the ingredients or something like that."

"That's right, I need to get her recipes. I have a couple of clients who'd like to start making it themselves too. Did she get a license to sell them or is she just making them for herself?"

Kai shrugs, "No idea. She hasn't said anything about it."

"So, are you two living together?" I can't believe I'm asking this. I must be some kind of masochist, but I'd rather know than have my imagination taking me places I don't want to go.

"Nah, she's staying at her parents' place while they're traveling."

"Oh. Okay, well, those dishes aren't going to do themselves." I get up and on my way to the kitchen, I tweak Ev's nose and whisper a "boop" like my mother used to do, making him look up and grin. And just like that, he's five again. My little brother, with dreams and bright eyes.

I've done everything I can to make sure our parents' deaths didn't kill that boyish side of him.

"Hey, Riv?"

"Yeah?" My eyes travel to his bright green ones, albeit droopy with pain meds.

"I love you, big sis. Thanks for taking care of me. And not just now, but always." I smile, my heart constricting with emotion.

"You're my number one." With a wink, I make my way to the kitchen as quickly as I can. I need a minute to gather my feelings up and process the last few days. I can survive a lot of things. I can handle all the shit coming my way. The stalkers, the weird phone calls, the severed members at my doorstep.

Kai getting engaged.

But losing my brother? I would never come back from that.

Mindlessly, I put all of our dishes into the machine that Ev hooked up to the well water. In fact, he's hooked everything that isn't drinking water to the well. Except for the laundry, since it makes the clothes dingy and slightly orange looking over time.

"Hey, you okay, Psyche?" I jump slightly at the sound of his voice right next to me. I was so deep in my thoughts that I didn't realize anyone had walked in.

"Oh, yeah. Just making sure everything is cleaned up so Petal doesn't have to worry about anything but her husband." I glance over at him before going back to washing the pan using the natural sponges Petal loves so much.

From the corner of my eye, I see him grabbing a towel, waiting to take the pots and pans from me so he can dry them off. It's such a domestic thing to do, it catches me off guard. In truth, the four of us—well, five if we count his fiancée—have always worked well together, knowing each other's limits and expectations. So why does this feel so damn awkward?

"We haven't really talked about it since..." My grip falters slightly on the wet dish but thankfully, I don't let it slip from my hold.

"Talk about what, exactly?" It's always best to make sure we're both on the same page. I'm assuming he's referring to Freya and their sudden engagement, but for all I know he's talking about my brother's accident.

"The engagement." Without sparing him a glance, I pass the dish to him and go back to lathering up another pot.

"What's there to talk about?" I smile. It's the only proper thing to do. "It's a simple story. Boy meets girl, boy fucks girl. They fall madly in love and get hitched. As old as time itself." He snorts. I frown but keep washing, meticulously.

"Right." At his tone, I stop everything and turn to face him—my wet, soapy hand on my hip—hoping he'll offer up more than just a one-word answer without added prompting. When he just stares back at me, a crooked grin making his dimples pop out, I fight everything in me not to laugh at his antics.

"You know what, Psyche? It's not like you to play coy." Shaking my head, I go back to my task. "I'm not playing anything. I'm just slowly figuring out that I really don't know much of anything anymore."

When I hand off the pot, his fingers wrap around my hand, his thumb caressing soft circles around the base of mine, his eyes having lost all mirth.

"I promise, you'll know everything..."

"I'm going to make some magnolia tea to help Ev sleep." Petal breezes in like a wife on a mission, oblivious to the tension in the kitchen.

Kai is the first to react, his attention zeroed in on Petal.

"Isn't the morphine enough?" All confusion about promises and knowing everything is gone, my worry about Everest spiking once more.

"I thought he'd be asleep by now." Petal reaches for a glass container, one of many tea ingredients that are neatly arranged in alphabetical order inside her cupboard. "We spoke with the doctor and decided that the strict minimum of morphine could be enough. We don't want him getting used to it." She takes out the thin layers of bark and carefully places them on a small plate then goes about heating the water.

"Is it safe? I mean, won't the pain be too much?" I'm worried now, of course, and because he's Kai, he places a hand at my nape and squeezes as though he wants to take my stress for himself.

"He'll be toking as well, but if he's in too much pain, we'll revisit the decision."

The fact that all possibilities are still on the table reassures me and for the first time, I can see the adult in her. Sure, technically she's been one for a while, but at this moment, she's taking charge to make sure her husband's wishes are respected.

Giving Kai a grateful smile, I finish up my dishes and go check on Everest.

Turns out, my brother needed the rest. He's been asleep for a couple of hours now, while Petal, Kai and I sit out back around the fire pit. It's cold but the fire and our winter jackets are keeping us warm.

"Did you ever find out who sent you a severed dick?" I choke on my tea when Petal asks me the question like she'd asked about the weather.

"What the fuck?" I sigh at Kai's immediate response. I guess I forgot to tell him. In my defense, he'd just announced he was getting married, so I suppose I was a little distracted.

Ignoring his outburst, I look to Petal as I bring the roach to my lips and take a small hit. "No, but I did get a phone call from the police saying they were still investigating. Apparently, the guy they fished out from the Hudson, the one missing his junk, was also missing his teeth." I'm not giving them anything more since, yes, I've actually met the fucker in question while he rearranged my face against a brick wall.

"Wait, back up." Kai is surprisingly alert when he leans his elbows on his knees and pins me with a look that's part confusion, part rage. "Someone sent you a dick? Like an actual person's cock?" Shaking his head like he's trying to reprogram his brain into telling something that makes more sense, he runs his hands through his hair and waits while I try to gather my thoughts.

It's not that I don't want to talk about it, but fucking hell, how many times do I have to tell this fucking story? Of course... I do. I tell him about the weird phone calls. The box at my doorstep. The police. The dead body missing a dick. Mostly, I tell him I have no fucking clue who's been terrorizing me.

Unfortunately, I'm on a roll, forgetting that I haven't told anyone about the next episode.

"You were attacked in a fucking alleyway? Jesus Christ, River. How are we just now hearing about this?" Kai's on his feet so quickly I don't have the time to register that he's coming toward me.

In seconds, I'm engulfed in his arms, surrounded by the addicting scent of sandalwood, and my body just melts into his heat.

"Fuck, Riv, I'm sorry I wasn't there for you." I just shrug because what could he have done anyway? And then it all comes back to me, clearly.

"Actually, you kinda were there. Do you remember trying to call me, a little over a month ago?" Kai pulls me away from him just enough so I can see the wheels turning in his weed-fogged mind.

"Maybe? I'm always trying to call you but you hardly ever fucking pick up, so..." He's not lying.

"Well, that night, when he grabbed me"—I shiver at the memory but continue my story—"my phone and keys fell on the sidewalk and it's because you kept calling me that a few strangers ended up in the alley and running off my attacker." Looking up at Kai, I feel this blanket of warmth cover me as his mouth breaks into a gorgeous, boyish grin. Dimples included.

"I'm glad I helped, in a way, but still... I wish I'd been there to kill that fucker and then take care of you." The sincerity and solemn promise in his voice is almost overwhelming. But I have to remind myself that sometimes he can be such a fucking douche canoe that needs to be chopped up and dropped in a river. I mean, he's my best friend and I love him, but I just told him that I'd been attacked by some random stranger in an alley, and his only concern is that he wasn't there to be a macho man fuck ass dick face. He can't even be bothered to ask me if I'm all right.

"It's okay, I ran into Nathaniel and he patched me right up." *See, I didn't even need you.*

No sooner do the words escape my mouth than Kai loses that relaxed way about him. Still holding me, he now feels stiff, like my words have frozen his spine into place.

"I can't believe you didn't tell us." Petal pouts, yet is looking at us with stars in her eyes as she curls up in the corner of the chair.

Kai releases me, leaning back just enough to place my long strands of hair behind my ear. I answer Petal but my eyes are fixed on Kai. "I didn't want to worry you. Besides," I turn to look at my sister-in-law and grin. "I'm a fucking survivor."

"You're a beautiful survivor, River, and we love you always."

Kai returns to his seat, but not before he takes my roach. "Hey!"

And just like that, we're back to normal. Until Kai, out of the fucking blue, announces—not asks—that he's going to teach me self-defense so the next time someone tries to attack me, I can kick their balls right up their throat.

"Since when do you know self-defense?" Mirroring Petal's position, I burrow into my coat as the chill begins to seep in. Seeing us, Kai runs to the woodshed and grabs a few logs to throw on the fire.

"I'm a man," he uses a voice that has some kind of wannabe southern thing going on, which makes us laugh until tears spring and threaten to fall down our cheeks. "We men know how to fight, little lady. It's innate and shit."

**CAG:** Hey beautiful, just wanted to check up on you and your brother.

**Me:** Hello handsome *kissy face emoji* we're good. Just call me Cindersister. Nothing glamorous about my lifestyle. *Farmer girl emoji*

**CAG:** Sounds like role play is in our future. *Devil emoji*

**Me:** I like the way you think. *Eggplant emoji*

**CAG:** I'll try to come by tomorrow after my last patients. I promise. Need to up my boyfriend game or else Cindersister might search for a Charming Farmer.

**Me:** You better hurry, time's a ticking. The Farmer's Ball is coming up soon.

I don't need to look in the mirror to know I have a goofy smile on my face. Nathaniel brings it out in me. Everything is just so easy with him. I just wish his patients would be less sick so I could have more of his time, but I suppose having a boyfriend—holy shit, I have a boyfriend?—who saves lives demands the sacrifice of his time.

"What are you smiling about, Psyche?" Kai brushes up next to me just when I slide my phone into my back pocket. The last week here at my brother's, I've hung up my designer clothes for plain old comfy jeans and warm sweaters. Crops don't give a fuck what you're wearing, but your Chanel and Louboutin's do care about where you step and kneel.

"Nothing, just Nathaniel checking in." Kai's jovial demeanor is gone in an instant.

"Right." I pick up my basket filled with dead plant matter and make my way to the compost. Kai cleaned it up yesterday, using the bottom for the soil.

"Come on, I'm freezing. Let's get some hot chocolate." From the corner of my eye, I see him shake his head slightly, like he's trying to rid himself of any negativity, and just when I turn fully toward him, he grants me a signature Kai Briggs grin, dimples and all.

"With marshmallows on top?"

"Is there any other way?" When he catches up to me, he takes my basket and empties it into the compost bin then puts the basket away on the wooden shelf he built for easy and organized access.

"Don't let Petal know we're eating industrialized or processed foods, she'll have a coronary." Kai's whispered words sound like we're conspiring against our parents, reminding me of when we were kids making trouble in our carefree world.

"It'll be our little secret." Swinging an arm around my shoulders, Kai leans in and kisses the top of my head like he's done a million times in our lives. His sandalwood scent dances under my nostrils with every step we take back to my brother's house as we joke about living in Prohibition times—the sugar version.

"So, I'm thinking..."

"Don't hurt yourself, buddy." Kai hip checks me as we walk.

"Don't be a brat." Then he places his soil-covered hand over my mouth to shut down my next quip. "After lunch, I'll teach you some simple and easy self-defense moves. I don't like the idea of you being in danger in the city with no one to help you if you're in trouble." Releasing my mouth so I can answer, he looks down on me expectantly.

"First of all, gross. You literally had your hands in dirt not five minutes ago and then placed that hand on my mouth." Kai shrugs like we've done worse.

We have.

"Second, I am not alone in the city, but yes, I would love to have a lesson or two on how to rip a dude's junk off." Visibly shuddering at my words, he squeezes me and grins down on me.

"I'll make you a lethal weapon, yet, little Psyche." We're looking at each other, grinning, when a familiar voice adds all the chill to the already cold morning air.

"Well, aren't we cozy?"

Kai looks up at Freya, and to my surprise, he doesn't let go of me but he does smile at her and greet her with fondness.

"Hey Frey, I was telling this crazy one that I'd give her some fighting skills, wanna join in on the fun?" Schooling her grimace into a polite smile, she sidles up to Kai, wrapping her arms around his waist and forcing him to let go of me, and tells us that she can't since her parents are due to be back in a couple of hours. They're passing through before heading back out toward the south.

We all have lunch in the living room so we can hang out with Everest and when we're done Freya heads home.

Petal stays with her husband to help him fall back asleep while we sneak in a hot chocolate with mini marshmallows, snickering like teenagers. Turns out, Kai has a jar of them hidden in a wooden panel inside Petal's cupboard. Along with other junk foods she wouldn't touch with a ten-foot pole.

Once outside, Kai is all business.

"You need to focus on the guy's vulnerable spots. Eyes, throat, groin, nose. The goal is maximum impact in the least amount of time. Basically, you're not there to have a five round boxing match with the dude. You want to hurt him enough that you can run. Got it?" He raises a brow, knowing damn well that running away goes against my nature. I'd want to finish the job once my attacker is on the ground. But he's right, so I nod with a very convincing, "Got it."

"Give me your house keys." I'd picked them up—at his request—when we walked out of the house. Digging into my back pocket, I hand them over and then jump up and down to warm up my body. It's too fucking cold to be outside but fuck it, I need to listen to Kai.

"There are two ways you use your keys while you're walking on the street. First, grip them like this." He places the keys in his palm, allowing for the longest part to peek out from the side of his fist. “It’s called a hammer strike, which is basically how you’re going to plant your keys in his vulnerable areas.” As though he’s pounding on a door, Kai repeats the move three times.

“Okay, that sounds easy enough.” I mimic him, and as I do, he places my legs a little better so I don’t lose my balance as I strike.

“Good. You can also use a lanyard and whip it at him but I feel it’s not as precise of a move. Your choice.” Yeah, I prefer the pounding gesture. Seems quick and efficient.

We go through a few more moves. I’d known about them but didn’t really know how to put them into action. The groin kick and heel palm strikes—perfect for the nose and throat—are classics.

“Okay, so let’s say he’s holding you in some kind of bear hug.” Kai steps behind me and wraps his arms around my chest. Fuck me, I’m supposed to be concentrating on getting free not reveling in his delicious scent. “What you want to do—“ When he stops abruptly, I turn to look up at him in confusion.

“Stop wiggling your ass, River.” His words are a growl, full of restraint and laced with lust. Oops.

“Sorry, it’s cold and you’re warm so... yeah. Okay. Sorry. Let’s do this.”

Clearing his throat, he repeats his last instructions and I try with everything in me to ignore the growing hard-on that's poking me in my lower back.

"The idea is to get low so you can create a space for yourself—" I do just that, but instead of freeing myself from his hold, my foot gets caught in a root and we both collapse to the frozen ground.

We grunt as we end up lying one on top of the other. With matching grins on our faces from the utter failure of that move, we're breathing hard, our chests heaving from the efforts when suddenly his eyes grow serious, his tongue peeking out and licking his lips. I do the same, like his actions cause a mirror effect on me.

The warmth of his body is heating my entire front, his leg between mine as his torso is held up by his elbows on either side of my head.

In that moment, everything grows still. There are no cars driving by, no children playing in the neighboring yards. No chattering passers-by. No car doors slamming.

In that moment, there's only Kai and me, not just looking, but boring into each other.

Faster than I could ever imagine, Kai's leaning down and his lips graze mine in a kiss so fucking soft it brings tears to my eyes.

Just then, an image of Nathaniel flashes in my mind and I use my palms and knees to apply every lesson Kai has just taught me by pushing him off me and jumping to my feet.

Looking down on him, I jump up and down, preferring to chalk up his actions as a self-defense lesson instead of analyzing what he's just done.

"I got away! Do I run now?"

The unmistakable sounds of foot falls catch my attention. Turning to the side, I see Nathaniel just as he slides his hands in the pockets of his slacks and heaves a breath of disappointment.

I panic.

"It's not what you think, Nathaniel. I swear we were just—"

"I think I see my girlfriend kissing the man she's loved her entire life. Am I wrong?"

Kai jumps to his feet and steps forward as though shielding me from the situation.

"Look, man, I'm sorry. I was just showing her some self-defense moves and—"

"And you thought you'd stick your tongue down her throat?" Shaking his head, he takes one last look at me and turns on his heel back toward his car.

"Nathaniel!" The shock finally evaporates long enough to get my feet moving, I run to the car and grip the door. "I... it was just a weird thing." I can't find the words to explain what just happened. It certainly wasn't planned and I didn't initiate any of it.

"I know, River. I saw it all. I know you didn't reciprocate but here's the thing." Placing a palm over my flushed cheek, he whispers just for me. "You need to look deep inside yourself, figure out what you really need and want. I'm all in, but I'm not going to play games and beat the shit out of the guy you've loved for the better part of your life." Leaning down, he places a soft, warm kiss on my forehead and before he gets back into his car to leave, he gives me his parting words.

"When your heart finally decides who it wants to belong to, you know where to find me. Or him."

# Chapter Fifteen
## Nathaniel

The drive from the ferry to River's brother's house is really peaceful for a Saturday afternoon. It's something Angelica would've enjoyed when she was alive. I've thought a lot about her lately, mainly what her reaction to what I'm doing would be. I'm not sure she would approve. In fact, I know she wouldn't. The thought doesn't make me feel good, but I can turn it around, do the right thing.

Pulling up on the gravel driveway outside Everest's house helps settle something inside me. I may not believe in all this mumbo jumbo crap that River's family does, but I can appreciate the beauty of it. It's definitely not what I expected when all this started.

*What the fuck?*

I have to be seeing things. A lump forms in my throat at what I'm witnessing.

Fucking Kai, on top of River, kissing her.

I guess the universe—or whatever the fuck Petal believes in—is causing a divine intervention.

This wasn't what was supposed to happen. It's all fucking fucked, but for some reason, I'm actually a little relieved.

*Fuck.*

Slowly getting out of the car, all I can do is watch, almost like it's happening in slow motion, as River pushes Kai away and jumps up, a beaming and beautiful fucking smile on her perfect face. The swirling hurt inside me wants to pummel Kai to the ground, but then River would see what kind of man I really am. And that was never the plan.

I let out a heavy sigh and put my hands in my pockets as River turns around. The look on her face when she sees me transforms from happy and carefree to sad and guilty.

"It's not what you think, Nathaniel. I swear we were just—"

"I think I see my girlfriend kissing the man she's loved her entire life. Am I wrong?"

Kai jumps to his feet and moves to stand in front of her, as if he's protecting her from me. As if I'm dangerous

*If only he knew.*

"Look, man, I'm sorry. I was just showing her some self-defense moves and—"

"And you thought you'd stick your tongue down her throat?" Shaking my head, I take one last look at River and turn on my heel back toward the car. Disappointment and regret flowing through my entire body makes this a lot harder than it should be.

This whole thing was a huge fucking mistake.

"Nathaniel!" River's shout makes me pause and turn to her as she reaches the car. "I... it was just a weird thing."

The furrow of her brow and sadness in her eyes are heartbreaking. I know she didn't mean for this to happen, but it did. And there's fuck all I can do about it.

"I know, River. I saw it all. I know you didn't reciprocate but here's the thing." Placing a palm over her flushed cheek, I whisper my next words because they're too difficult to get out fully. "You need to look deep inside yourself, figure out what you really need and want. I'm all in but I'm not going to play games and beat the shit out of the guy you've loved for the better part of your life." Leaning down, I place a soft, warm kiss on her forehead and before I get back into the car to leave. I give her my parting words.

And this time, I hope she chooses wisely.

"When your heart finally decides who it wants to belong to, you know where to find me. Or him."

With that, I climb into my car and drive away.

I've set her free, let her go.

Fate can decide the rest.

To Be Continued in

The Filthy One

Volume 3: The Escort

https://geni.us/TheFilthyOne

# The Blonde One

This writing journey is epic. The Brunette One truly is a pleasure to work with! So much so, it doesn't feel like we're working at all. After the success and great feedback from The Rich One, we're in a constant excitable mood. These men are all hot hot hot! And so much fun to write, we hope you enjoyed our Kinky Elijah and his supporting wife. The best things can happen when we step out of our comfort zones and try something new!

Thank you to all the readers giving our books a chance, and thank you to the authors who are including us with their release parties. We also have grown a special place in our dark little hearts for the Dehydrated Bitches Facebook group. Thank you for having us!

I'm all full of gratitude right now, much like Petal usually is! For the people who know who we are, we are eternally grateful for what you do for us. For the people who haven't figured it out, we are eternally grateful for your faith in us and your support.

Also really want to thank our families for putting up with our constant zoom calls and time spent away from them so we can write all the words and discuss all the things! And boy… do we have some things in store!!

For now, I'll leave you with a teeny hint… as promised…

The Brunette One and I… have pets.

Yup, I know… huge hint there!! ;)

Actually… since writing this… my little Pom is not with us anymore.

# The Brunette One

I'm not sure how I'm supposed to top the Blond One's kind words. What I can say is that this adventure is everything I love about writing. I love the late night talks as we plot the demise of... well, pretty much everyone. The groans every time we mention the word "blurb". The anticipation of putting another one of our babies out for the world to read. It's all great, it's all exciting and I don't think there could be a better match for me as a co-author. My Other One is the best and she's ALL MINE.

# Books by N.O. One

## Dark Romance

**The Escort Series (MF)**

The Rich One ~ https://geni.us/TheRichOne

The Kinky One ~ https://geni.us/TheKinkyOne

The Filthy One ~ https://geni.us/TheFithyOne

The Broken One ~ https://geni.us/TheBrokenOne

The Almost One ~ https://geni.us/TheAlmostOne

The Forever One ~ https://geni.us/TheForeverOne

**KOK (RH)**

Kings of Kink ~ https://geni.us/KingsOfKink

**The Reapers Mafia Crew Duet (MF)**

One Kill ~ https://geni.us/TheReapers1

One Love ~ https://geni.us/TheReapers2

**The Psycho Trilogy – Sons of Khaos (MF)**

Psycho Hate ~ https://geni.us/PsychoHate

Psycho Love ~ https://geni.us/PsychoLove

Psycho Reign ~ https://geni.us/PsychoReign

**A Night To Remember Auction – A shared world (MF)**

Once Upon A Sale ~ https://geni.us/OnceUponASale

Books in the Auction Shared world by other authors ~ https://www.amazon.com/dp/B0CLKVXLXJ

**Sons of Khaos – The Standalones**

Bear Hunt (MF) ~ https://geni.us/SOKBearHunt

If you'd love to get in touch or find out more about our books, please feel free to stalk us in all the places and join our newsletter.

www.author-no-one.com

If you'd love to get in touch or find out more about our books, please feel free to stalk us in all the places and join our newsletter.

Here is our linktree: https://linktr.ee/n.o.one

# BOOKS WE THINK YOU SHOULD READ

# Dark Romance

DATE WITH THE DEVIL (MF) ~
HTTPS://GENI.US/DWTD

## Contemporary

THE UCC SAGA

DISHEVELED ~ HTTP://AMZN.TO/2ARPBXP

DISARMED ~ HTTP://AMZN.TO/2MYVXNN

DISCARDED ~ HTTPS://AMZN.TO/2VWTRPF

UCC BOXSET ~ HTTPS://AMZN.TO/3LJVEPE

STANDALONE

THE WISH ~ HTTPS://AMZN.TO/2FTIKQB

## Rom-Com

THE WOOLF FAMILY SERIES

SCREWED ~ HTTPS://GENI.US/SCREWED

SCREWED UP ~ HTTPS://BIT.LY/3IBFWKB

SCREWED OVER (COMING SOON)

## Supernatural

SOUL GUARDIANS SERIES

REPRISE ~ HTTPS://BIT.LY/3CT9NPE

el

Eva LeNoir

Fun Flirty Romance

# BY LILY WILDHART

## Dark Romance

**The Saints of Serenity Falls series (RH)**

(You will find crossovers from The Escort series by N.O. One in the Serenity Falls series by Lily Wildhart, and vice versa!)

A Burn So Deep ~ https://geni.us/burnaltcover

A Revenge So Sweet ~ https://geni.us/revengealtcover

A Taste Of Forever ~ https://geni.us/tastealtcover

# Other Hudson Indie Ink Authors

## Paranormal Romance/Urban Fantasy

Stephanie Hudson

Tatum Rayne

Xen Randell

Sorcha Dawn

Georgia Seren Mills

## Crime/Action

Blake Hudson

Jack Walker

## Contemporary Romance

Gemma Weir

Nikki Ashton

Nicky Priest

Jax Knight

N.O. One

Website & Newsletter: www.author-no-one.com

Facebook: https://geni.us/Facebookauthor

Facebook Group: https://geni.us/FierceReaders

Instagram: https://geni.us/Instagramauthor

Goodreads: https://geni.us/Goodreadsauthor

Bookbub: https://www.bookbub.com/profile/n-o-one

Linkedtree https://linktr.ee/n.o.one

www.ingramcontent.com/pod-product-compliance
Ingram Content Group UK Ltd.
Pitfield, Milton Keynes, MK11 3LW, UK
UKHW042104240925
8055UKWH00040B/73

9 781917 471015